A WINTER OF DISCONTENT FOR HENRY MILCH

THE WYANDOT COUNTY MYSTERIES
BOOK 4

MARSHALL THORNTON

Published by Kenmore Books

Edited by Joan Martinelli

Cover design by Marshall Thornton

Images by 123rf stock

ISBN: 978-1-965306-08-6

 Created with Vellum

ACKNOWLEDGMENTS

A big thank you to: Joan Martinelli, John Adams, Dale B., Tina Greene Bevington, Danielle Wolfe, Ben Thompson and Jennie Evenson.

CHAPTER ONE

Babies are disgusting. Oh, I know we're all supposed to think they're adorable and cuddly and 'don't the tops of their heads just smell marvelous.' But the reality is different. They never sleep when you want them to—they're meant to sleep at least fourteen hours a day (look it up on Yahoo! it's correct), but somehow it's never a convenient fourteen hours. They're constantly crying for at least fifteen of the ten hours they're awake and, worst of all, when they *are* awake it's mostly about sour smelly stuff going in and sour smelly stuff coming out. Repeatedly. Over and over again. Every. Single. Day.

Honestly, I don't understand how humankind has survived this long, given the temptation to put the baby down, walk away, and never think about them again. Oh stop, I wouldn't actually do it... But my god, the temptation!

Luckily, when my mother abandoned Emerald, my baby sister, with my Nana Cole and me, my grandmother's friends Jan, Bev, Dorothy and Barbara stepped up and helped. Jan had even gotten a large sheet of card stock from Staples in Traverse and drawn a big grid with 31 days. Using colored Post-it notes and glitter pens—she couldn't resist those—the ladies divided up which days they'd come help, which was most. It had been working well enough for a bit more than five months.

I guess we'd have gotten less help if my Nana Cole wasn't still iffy on her feet. She'd had a stroke last spring, which might or might not have been my fault, and had never fully recovered. There was the very real possibility she'd drop the baby into a pot of boiling water. Everyone thought that was a bad idea—even me.

Usually, we had help in the afternoon for three or four hours, which meant I could take a nap. Which is what I was doing that day in late January, sleeping on my stomach, snoring lightly, drool running down my cheek, when my cell phone chirped.

"It's Ham."

"Mmmghhh..."

Ham was Hamlet Gilbody, a private eye with an office down in Grand Rapids. I'd kind of saved his life when he was in Masons Bay the previous September, and he'd offered me a part time job. Since I'd been planning to head back to Los Angeles—and still was—I'd turned him down.

But then my mother pulled her disappearing act and abandoned my sister—words like that annoy my Nana Cole, so I use them as often as possible. She prefers words like 'left' or 'entrusted': My mother entrusted my sister to our care. I prefer dumped, flaked, bailed, took a powder, and most reliably, abandoned. When she *abandoned* my sister, I was forced to stay at the farm, at least a little while longer, so I contacted Hamlet Gilbody, PI, around Thanksgiving and accepted his offer.

"Were you asleep?" he asked. "It's the middle of the afternoon."

"There's a baby in the house, remember? I have to sleep when I can."

"Oh. Well. *Can* you work? I have a job for you."

"Yeah, I can work. What's the job?"

There was no way I was turning it down. It was the first

one he'd offered. Really, I thought he was never going to call again. Yeah, yeah, yeah… it would probably be difficult to juggle the baby and my grandmother and the job, but I needed to do something that brought in money and didn't include changing diapers or watching *Hannity & Colmes*.

"A woman named Roberta LaCross. Goes by Bobbie. She's around seventy. She went to a winery up that way, fell in the bathroom, and broke her arm. Claims she was overserved."

Okay, that was disappointing. There had to be more exciting jobs than that. An old lady got drunk and broke her arm. What needed to be investigated? I tried to point that out. "You can't fake a broken arm, she either broke it or she didn't."

"Something about it seems off. For one thing, it's not her first time at the rodeo."

"What rodeo?"

"She's litigious. I got one of her former neighbors on the phone and apparently this lady breaks bones all the time."

"She's old."

"You're right. She's old and bad things keep happening to her. And maybe that's it. And maybe it's not. I'm going to email you the file and you let me know what you think. Okay?"

"Sure."

I mean, seriously, he'd pay me for my opinion? How could I turn that down? As promised, the email with the file arrived a few minutes later. I printed it out. I didn't have to do that, but I'd moved back into my mother's old bedroom and was using the French Provincial desk she'd had as a teenager. I'd bought some Pendaflex files for the bottom drawer and was excited about finally filling them up.

There were a handful of questions I hadn't asked and probably should have. For one, who was his client? That was answered by the first two pages that came out of my printer. They were the contract with the client. In this case, it was Midwest Property, Casualty and Life. The agreement laid out how much Ham was being paid. He'd wisely blacked that out before scanning the document, so I knew it was a lot more than I was getting. Wait—how much *was* I getting? I hadn't asked. I should have asked. Well, it was more than the nothing I'd be making if I turned it down, so it probably didn't matter much.

The contract also provided a brief description of what was to be investigated. 'On August 13th, 2002, Roberta LaCross claims she was overserved at Three Friends winery in Wyandot Township, fell in the ladies' room after slipping on a puddle of water and broke her arm.'

Pretty much what Ham had said. The next thing out of my printer was the six-page lawsuit Roberta LaCross had filed. Her attorneys were Straub and Straub, whose office was on Main Street in Masons Bay. The suit laid out the same story, pretty much, though it used more sinister adjectives and tried to make it seem like the staff at Three Friend's had forced the alcohol onto their client with "aggressive" sales techniques. And that the water on the bathroom floor was clear evidence of negligence. She was asking a million dollars for damages and emotional distress. That seemed excessive. I mean, she had to be on Medicare, and she probably didn't work. Right? She wouldn't need to be reimbursed for either medical expenses or lost wages. So that was a million dollars just for pain and suffering. That's a lot of pain and suffering.

Next was the emergency room report on her injury. She had a displaced oblique fracture of the humerus just below the left shoulder joint. Surgery was not indicated. She was told to wear a sling at all times and remain as still as possible. She was also given a prescription for Oxy. A generous one. With refills.

Lucky lady.

The report included her X-rays, which printed out as dark blobs. They were easier to see on my iBook G3. Honestly, it looked a whole lot worse than it sounded. The bone had split into two jagged pieces that were floating near each other but not connected. It looked very painful.

After that were pages of interviews with the workers at the

winery, Roberta's two friends who were with her, and Roberta herself. I was too sleepy to read through the interviews just then, so I stacked them next to the printer. There was more stuff in the file, but I didn't bother looking at it. I just printed it out and then stuck the whole mess in a manila folder, which went into a Pendaflex. I felt very efficient.

After a brief cat nap, I went downstairs; I actually was very excited. I was going to be an investigator. Like Angel on TV. Except not a vampire. And hotter. In a boyish way. I did hope I could wrap this up in a well-structured hour—and then charge for six.

In the kitchen, Nana Cole sat with Bev and Barbara. Both were close friends of hers. Bev was younger than Nana Cole, had steel gray hair like a brush and a sharp nose that might cut you if you got too close. Barbara was closer to my grandmother's age, with wispy hair and a sweet personality. Bev was jiggling Emerald in her arms and trying to get her to take a bottle. It was a chore. Lately, Emerald had been pushing the bottle away. Not because she wasn't hungry, simply because she could. Frustrating people seemed to delight her.

"Here comes the choo-choo train," Bev said, adding in a few sounds that distracted Emeral enough to get the bottle into her mouth.

We'd started out trying to keep her on a strict feeding schedule, Nana Cole's idea, feeding her every four hours, which meant seven, eleven, three, seven, eleven and most nights 3 a.m. That schedule crumbled quickly, and feedings happened willy-nilly. When she cried or otherwise fussed, I had a three-word mantra: stinky, sleepy, hungry. If she'd slept recently and didn't need a diaper change, then she was probably hungry. I glanced at the clock which said 4:34. See what I mean? Willy-nilly.

"I got a job," I announced.

"A what?" Nana Cole asked.

"Why did you get a job?" Bev asked. "You have a job. You said you just needed a break to take care of Emerald."

I did, in fact, say that. Mostly because I didn't want to work for the Wyandot County Land Conservancy anymore. It turns out tromping around fields with grumpy farmers isn't my idea of fun.

"I'm going to be a private investigator."

"Oh, don't be ridiculous," Nana Cole said. "You're the last person—"

"Excuse me. You *paid* me to find out who killed Reverand Hessel."

"And how well did that go?"

"It's complicated."

I did find his killer. Sue Langtree. But she'd framed her granddaughter's rapist, Donny Hyslip, so I left it alone. Or at least I did for a while. Last fall, I gave Detective Lehmann a tip that led to her arrest, but Nana Cole didn't know any of that. All she knew was that I hadn't caught Donny Hyslip, and I hadn't caught Sue Langtree.

"Emma, you should be proud of Henry," Barbara said. "He *does* try. And he's so good with little Emerald."

I could tell Nana Cole wanted to snort, but she restrained herself. "I suppose this job is through that Hamish fellow down in Grand Rapids."

"Hamlet."

"I can't imagine why he thinks—"

"I saved his life. He owes—"

"Oh, pishposh. That's an overstatement. I don't see what Nancy Fisher's drowning has to do with him."

"I saved him from her nephew."

"Elbert Robins wouldn't hurt a fly." Now I was sorry he'd taken a plea deal. If there'd been a trial, I could have dragged Nana Cole there every day and plunked her in the front row. Let her pishposh that.

"He killed Dr. Blinski. He admitted it."

"Well, no one's perfect."

I'd had about enough of that. I wasn't sure how serious Nana Cole was anyway. Sometimes she said things because she'd like them to be true, no matter how obvious it was that they weren't. And sometimes she said things just to annoy me. Seriously, she needed to get out more.

"I have to work tomorrow afternoon," I said, walking over to the chart hanging on the wall next to. "Do you think Jan might stay an extra hour or two?"

"I'll call her," Bev said.

"And if she won't do it, we will," Barbara said. And then she began to make goo-goo-ga-ga noises at the baby. I know that's supposed to help babies pick up language, but seriously, it makes adults look like idiots.

"Okay, well, thanks."

A few minutes later Bev and Barbara left, and it was time for Emerald's bath. I held onto her while the pink plastic tub filled up with warm water. She was a big baby. Over ten pounds when she was born and now nearly twenty. Heavier than a bowling ball. Which amused me: my sister, the bowling ball.

Nana Cole brought me a towel and the bar of Ivory soap she insisted we use. I had to do the shopping, of course, so I'd gone ahead and bought some baby-specific soap, organic even, but she'd thrown it away and I had to use what she'd used on me and my mother.

"Do you want to go to a meeting later?" she asked. "The baby can watch TV with me. We'll be fine."

I wanted to slap her, but I couldn't put Emerald down just then. She was wiggling too much, and saying na, na, na. I could tell she was on her way to the word 'no'. She didn't want to get in the bath. She never wanted to get into the bath even though she liked it once she was in.

"I'm fine."

There is no planet on which I would admit to my Nana

Cole that I'd ever gone to a meeting. Despite the fact that NA was supposed to be anonymous—I mean it's in the name for god's sake—someone had gossiped about the few times I'd gone, and it had gotten back to my grandmother. Now she was always asking me about it.

She spread the towel out on the counter, and I laid Emerald down so I could undress her. My grandmother waddled off to get a clean onesie. Emerald's room was upstairs; or at least her crib was. She slept in the second bedroom I'd used when my mother was here. I'd flipped the bed up against the wall, and put in the crib and a table with things she might need at night. Other than that, most of her things were downstairs. Basically, the entire house had been turned into a nursery.

Once Emerald was naked, I dipped her into the three inches of warm water. She giggled as her butt touched it—see, she *did* like a bath.

I said, "Uh-huh, you likey washy, washy, baby-waby."

And then I heard myself and thought, *Oh crap.*

CHAPTER TWO

Pretty much everything from the time my mother *abandoned* us until around Thanksgiving is a blur. I was probably a zombie, and I've never heard anyone say zombies have good memories, so there you go. I'd gotten a prescription for Ativan and, as promised, it smoothed over the edges of withdrawal. Or at least I think it did. Taking care of a new baby and quitting Oxy are not as different as you'd think: anxiety, sleep disturbance, yawning, body aches, vomiting (only twice), shaking and rapid breathing. See? Hard to tell which was causing all that.

To be fair, we did have a lot of help the first few weeks. The baby bunch, as I began to think of them, was there for a lot of that time, changing diapers, feeding Emerald, swaddling her, rocking her, and just about anything else they could think of... *and* they brought food. Massive amounts. Not that I could eat much of it, but it did make it easier to feed Nana Cole. All too soon, they weren't coming as often and most of Emerald's care fell to me and my grandmother. Well, me.

I had significant, and logical concerns about leaving Nana Cole alone with my sister. Mostly, I was afraid she'd drop the baby and, as nearly as I could tell, infants don't bounce. A theory I did not want to test.

Eventually, I found what I thought might be a solution. Nana Cole had most of my mother's baby things, and most of mine. In the sixties, she'd used what amounted to a picnic basket to carry my infant mother around. Hard no. And in the eighties, she'd driven me around in a car seat that looked more like a gaming chair than anything that might protect a child. After assessing the situation, I did the reasonable thing and stole my grandmother's credit card from her purse. FYI: Theft for a good cause is completely moral. Ask Jean Valjean.

Anyhoo... I snatched the card, went to Target, and got the most expensive baby car seat/carrier they had. It had the word 'system' in its name, so it seemed perfect. It had a handle so you could secure the baby indoors and then carry the whole contraption out to the car. And then, if it was a nice day, you could carry your baby around with you—or at least that's what it showed on the box. It looked sturdy as a tank—well, as tank-like as molded plastic can be.

And, of course, Emerald hated it.

It wasn't terrible when I used the car seat in the car. The visual stimulation and the movement all kept Emerald amused (or terrified into silence, I'm not sure I could tell the difference) for long periods. But, when I'd set the car seat on the kitchen table, or anywhere else that wasn't moving, I'd have maybe five minutes before she started to fuss and ten before she outright began to scream. Which didn't mean I wasn't bound and determined that my plan would work.

The day after Ham's call, an hour before Jan arrived for her shift I got the baby into the car seat and left her with Nana Cole, while I went upstairs to make a call to the only actual almost friend I'd made since I got to Michigan nearly a year ago, Opal.

"Do you need a ride?" she asked when she picked up.

"No. I have a car."

"I've seen your car. 'Do you need a ride?' is a legitimate question."

You can probably see where the 'almost friend' part comes in. I snapped back, "Your car is an insect with eyelashes."

Opal drove a new Beetle with black plastic eyelashes on the headlights. She'd named it Ladybug. And that wasn't the worst of her crimes. About my age, she was a bisexual prone to abusing hair dye. Not that the two are connected. Bisexual people don't dye their hair anymore often... Whatever. The point is, from time to time, my almost friend Opal proved useful.

"What *do* you want?" she asked.

"I need to go to Three Friends winery and thought you might want to go with me. I'll drive."

"Why do you *need* to go to a winery?"

"I'm a private investigator."

"Is that a joke?"

"Is it funny?"

"Kind of."

"I just don't want to look suspicious."

"Are we going undercover?"

"No. I just don't want to scream PI."

"I can imagine a situation where you might scream but not one in which you'd look like a PI."

"Do you want to come or not?"

"Yeah, I've gotta see this."

Downstairs, as I was putting on my boots, I said to Nana Cole, "Jan will be here in five minutes. Don't touch the baby."

Ignoring me, she said, "Check the mail on your way out."

"Fine," I said, though I didn't want to do that. Our mailbox was at the end of our very long driveway on M-22. In the summer it was a pleasant little walk—birds and sunlight, and wildflowers at the curb. But in the winter. Well... you didn't just walk down there.

I got into my car—a popsicle blue, eleven-year-old Geo

Metro convertible—which was frigid inside. Not because the heater didn't work, it did, it just didn't work well enough to keep up with the hole in the canvas top. I drove to the end of the driveway and jumped out to get the mail.

It was snowing lightly, or maybe it was just the wind picking up snow and redepositing it. The lake had formed a crusty edge of ice, which the heaving waves kept breaking up. It was cold and desolate and made me feel like I was in a Bronte novel. And those never ended well.

I snatched the mail from the box and brought it back to my car. Nothing interesting. Our power bill, one of my credit cards telling me my payment was late, and a brochure from a local funeral parlor. I'd make sure to pass that along to Nana Cole.

Driving over the six inches of snow crumbles the plow had tossed into our driveway, I headed toward Masons Bay, about a ten-minute drive. When I got to the quaint village, Opal was standing in front of Pastiche where she worked. The first thing I noticed was that she was wearing a lavender faux fur coat that I wanted to steal and her hair was covered in a big, bulky pink hat. I was curious to see what color it was underneath. In the past, it had been orange, purple, green and yellow, and black and white (squares). I had no idea what she was going to do with it next.

The hat, though annoying, was necessary since it was about fifteen degrees. I myself was wearing my grandfather's corduroy hunting cap with ear flaps hanging down. I looked like a chic Bassett hound.

"Don't you have gloves?" she asked me, as I pulled away from the curb.

"I lose them." Mostly because I put them down and then don't bother to look for them. I mean, there was a vent on each side of the steering wheel so I could warm my hands up if it got really cold. Which reminded me, and so one at a time I held my hands over the vent.

"You don't have a scarf either."

"My scarf is... somewhere." Not a brilliant thing to say, everything is somewhere. "You know, I don't really think in those terms. I'm a Californian. Through and through."

"Remind me not to go to the Arctic with you."

"Unless George Bush starts exiling gay people to the Arctic, I will *never* go there."

"You know, if you get frostbite they cut your fingers off."

"Shut up."

Could you get frostbite when the temperature was, like, in the teens? I had no idea. I'd have to look it up on the Internet when I got home. If I still had fingers.

"So, Henry Milch, PI, what's the case?"

"An old lady fell down in the bathroom and now she's suing for a million dollars."

"Ouch."

"Yeah, that's what she said when she broke her arm."

Three Friends winery had once been a farm of some sort. Sitting in the midst of a snow-covered twenty or twenty-five acres, was a quaint farmhouse similar to my Nana Cole's: a wooden barn and a brand-new pole barn. The original barn had been converted into a tasting room.

A few days before, it had been close to forty and then quickly dropped well below freezing. The dirt parking lot had frozen into deep ridges. As Opal and I picked our way over to the tasting room, she said, "I think it's warmer outside than it is in your car."

"It is not," I said, though she might have been right.

I opened the glass door that led into the tasting room. On one side of the large room there were several banquet-sized tables, on the other a bar. The room was bright and sunny, large glass windows had been cut into the barn wall and looked out at the snow-covered vineyard. Most importantly, it was warm, very warm. There was a fireplace in one corner crackling away.

"Let's sit at a table," Opal said.

I ignored her and walked over to the bar, slipped off my puffer jacket and put it on the back of a stool. I was wearing a lime green sweater I'd found at a resale shop. I had to make some concession to the weather. And my grandfather's clothes, though they fit and were usually well made, were mostly gray and brown.

Grumbling, Opal crawled onto the stool next to me and wiggled out of her faux fur coat.

"I wanted to sit by the fire."

I shrugged.

There weren't a lot of 'tasters' at that moment. An older couple at a table and three middle-aged women at the bar. Behind the bar was a thickset woman with broad shoulders and curly blond hair. Loitering nearby was a girl who looked young enough to make me wonder if she should legally be there.

The barmaid—winemaid?—gave us tasting menus.

"We also have mulled wine."

"I'll have that," Opal said.

The woman looked at me. I shook my head. I couldn't stand mulled wine. It was like drinking a cinnamon flavored puddle.

"I'll go get that and let you look at the menu."

At the top of the menu was a photograph of two men and a woman in their twenties, and the story of how they went to college at U of M and decided to open a winery together. There was more to it than that, but I was just skimming. I was pretty sure the woman in the photo was the winemaid who'd handed us the menu. She wasn't aging especially well.

There were seven kinds of wine to try: three white, two reds, a rosé and a cherry wine. You could get a glass or you could get a flight, which was a taste of three different wines. I decided to get a flight and try all three of the white wines.

That prompted me to look around the large room again.

There were no buckets that I could see. This wasn't a tasting room where you spit the wine out. I suppose that made it more of a swallowing room.

"You're paying for this, aren't you?" Opal asked.

"It's not like I have a lot of money."

And I didn't. I was sneaking this onto my grandmother's credit card. Of course, she figured out I'd stolen it and then said I could keep it. For *household* expenses only. A definition I stretched when necessary; and it was often necessary.

"You don't have an expense account?"

Honestly, I had no idea. I hadn't asked.

The winemaid came back with Opal's mulled wine and I ordered my flight. Before the woman left, I said, "I'm Henry Milch, I work—"

"Emily Cole's son?"

"Yes. That's who I am. I'm—"

"We buy cherries from your grandmother."

"You do? But I thought her cherries were made into maraschinos?"

"She grows more than one kind." She looked at me like I was an idiot. "We buy her Ulsters for our cherry dessert wine."

"Oh, okay." Then I said, "Jasper Kaine does all that for my grandmother." That way I didn't sound like too much of an idiot. "I'm working for Hamlet Gilbody. Are you Melody Frasier?"

"I am. But it's Melanie."

"Sorry." I'd written down the names of the people who worked at the winery on the back of coffee receipt and put in my pocket, where it still was. "Uh... Hamlet is the investigator for your insurance company. He wanted me to look into the Roberta LaCross'... um, incident."

"Yeah, lemme get your flight. Then we'll talk."

She took a few steps away from us. Opal gave me the side-eye and said "Smooth," under her breath.

"Shut up."

When Melanie came back, she had this kind of carved wooden carrier which held three glasses partly filled with white wine. She set the contraption in front of me. Moving left to right, she said, "Chardonnay, Pinot Gris, and Late Harvest Reisling."

"Thank you. So, I've read your statement. I thought I'd go over a couple of things."

"If it will help, sure."

"Before she came in that afternoon, did you know Roberta?"

"Yes and no. I've seen her around, but I don't think we ever really met. I think the LaCross family is up in Leelanau County."

That was the county above us. The Pinky, as some people say. I didn't know much about it. I'd barely figured out Wyandot County.

"So, you were aware of her but not acquainted."

"I guess. Most of the people I know that age are in my family."

"What did you think of her? When she came in? First impression?"

"She was trying to look a lot younger than she is. Her hair was dyed, like a carrot color. And not in a punk way. More in an 'ooops, that didn't work out' way."

Opal chose that moment to take off her hat and fluff out her short hair. It was bright, a bright carrot color. Melanie looked over, saw her mistake, and covered by saying, "Yeah, but yours is deliberate. And believe it or not, looks more natural."

Natural was not what Opal had been going for. She said, "You said she was old. If her hair is white underneath, a color like red can fade quickly. And if she did it herself, she might not have prepped it correctly."

Melanie said, "It wasn't just her hair, it was the way she dressed. She had on this blue jean miniskirt. Like it was the nineteen sixties! And I swear she was wearing a push-up bra. Showed a lot of cleavage. Wrinkly cleavage."

"She claims she was overserved. Do you have her check?"

"Her friend paid. In cash. Which means we really have no idea at this point. I usually notice if people drink a lot, and I don't think she did."

"She was with two friends. Do you remember what time they got here?"

"It was early. We open at noon; she and her friends were here by one."

"What time did she fall?"

"Three-ish, I think. We called an ambulance, so about ten minutes before they arrived."

"That means she had two hours to be overserved."

"Yeah, see… in order to get drunk in that amount of time they'd have had to have ordered bottles. At least two." Melanie had clearly thought about this. "I'm sure they were drinking flights and single glasses."

I reached into my pocket and took out the slip of paper I'd written names on. She was right. Her name was Melanie. I asked, "What about Kylie Stark and Penny Pellitier? Are they here?"

"No. They don't even work here anymore. Penny bought the bookstore in Masons Bay and I think Kylie is working at the Walmart in Traverse City."

I had their contact information in the file, so I didn't need to ask. "They both interacted with Ms. LaCross?"

"They were here, but I was the one who served her party."

I took a sip of the Chardonnay while I tried to think of other questions to ask. The wine wasn't bad. Not that I'm a connoisseur.

"Wait, I thought some guy bought the bookstore?" I vaguely remembered my mother talking to him at a party. Not that it had anything to do with this.

"Joel Fletcher," Opal said. "He crashed and burned

around Thanksgiving. He thought he was going to make a mint selling books by Bill O'Reilly and Ann Coulter."

"My grandmother loves them."

"And how many books does she buy?"

Other than three copies of the Bible and one copy of *The Joy of Cooking*, there weren't a lot of books in Nana Cole's house.

"Penny got the business for a song," Melanie said.

"I think I'd like to see the ladies' room," I said. "You know, like, where it happened."

"Sure, go ahead."

"You don't want to check and see if anyone's in there?"

"No one's in there. It's not crowded; I can count."

I hopped off the stool and walked to the back of the room where the restrooms were. I opened the door to the ladies' room and walked in. I hadn't realized it, but Opal was right behind me.

The room looked more like the bathroom in most homes. It was meant for one person at a time. There was no stall, just an open toilet and a sink. There was a vase with plastic flowers on the back of the toilet, alongside a Lysol spray can. In case you stank up the place.

"Did she fall off the toilet?" Opal asked.

"No." Her statement was still fresh in my mind. "She said that after she used the toilet she fell on her way to the sink. That there was water on the floor, and she thinks she slipped."

"It's not a very big room."

I'd noticed that since we were kind of crammed together.

"I think if I started to fall, I'd just grab the sink."

"Even if you were drunk? Maybe she tried to and it didn't work," I suggested.

The door opened and Melanie stood in it. "What do you think?"

"How was she discovered?" I was particularly proud of that question. It sounded very *Law and Order*.

"She was screaming her head off. Her friends heard her and came in."

"Did you come to see what was happening?"

"Yeah. She was whimpering, moaning, howling. Very dramatic." After a moment, she added, "Sorry. I had more sympathy before she sued me."

"But she's not really suing *you*," Opal said. "Your insurance company is going to pay."

"There's a cap on the policy at three hundred thousand. If she gets the million she's asking for, the winery goes out of business."

"Can we get back to what happened?" I suggested. "Did you notice if there was water on the floor?"

"There was some water on the floor."

"How often do you and your staff check the restrooms?"

She gave me a grumpy look that said they didn't check often. "We don't know how the water got on the floor, or when. It could have gotten onto the floor when she fell."

"That doesn't make sense," I said. "In her statement, she says that she slipped on the way to the sink."

"No. When I came in the faucet was running. If I had to guess, I'd say she fell while washing her hands."

"People don't just fall down while washing their hands," I said. Though to be completely honest, I may have done it myself once or twice. A taste for opioids isn't all fun and games.

"She's an old lady," Opal said. "She could have had a ministroke. She could have fainted for a dozen reasons. Breaking her arm may be covering up whatever really happened."

I didn't know what really happened, obviously. All I knew was that Roberta's statement wasn't entirely correct. Or Melanie's wasn't. One of them wasn't telling the truth.

We went back to the bar. I was pretty sure I'd asked all my questions. Without asking me, Opal ordered a glass of wine for herself—the Late Harvest Reisling. I was about to tell her she was paying for it, when she asked, "You remember Carl Burke, don't you?"

"Yeah, the guy you're hopelessly in love with."

"I'm not— You're an ass." For some reason she didn't let that stop her. "Carl has this thing with Denny Hazzard."

"Who's that?"

"The barber."

"Oh him, yeah." I'd kissed him once. Not a fond memory. "What about him?"

"Have you seen him at any meetings? He told Carl he's off meth, but it's hard to believe."

Anger ripped through me like a flash flood. How did she know— "What meetings? I don't go to any meetings."

"You were seen. Everyone knows about it."

"Everybody's wrong. It must have been someone else."

"Someone else who dresses like you and calls himself Mooch?"

"It's possible."

"Look, have you seen Denny there or not?"

Occasionally, though it's rare, the truth will get you out of a sticky situation. I said, "I've been three times, and I haven't seen him. Why can't your 'sources' tell you if he's going?"

Ignoring that, she asked, "Did you go to the LGBT meeting?"

"I didn't know there was such a thing."

"Thursday nights at seven. They all go to Drip afterward. Maybe you could go and see if Denny is there."

"Why don't you go?"

"I'm not a drug addict."

"They don't test you at the door."

"I don't want to violate people's privacy."

"Seriously? You're literally gossiping about who's going. That's violating people's privacy."

"I was gossiping out of concern for Denny."

"Doing bad things for good reasons... You get a gold star."

She downed the rest of her wine, and got off the stool and put her fuzzy coat back on. Then she pulled her hat on and said, "I'll wait outside."

I put my coat on and paid before I followed her out to the parking lot. It had only been a couple of minutes, but her cheeks were already pink. Or maybe that was the wine.

Once we were in the car and I was about to start the engine, she said, "Oh, and by the way, there's baby puke all over the right shoulder of that sweater."

CHAPTER THREE

When I walked into the kitchen, Emerald was squirming in Jan's arms. She picked me out and smiled at me. Whether she knew it was me or not, I wasn't sure. I was getting the feeling she liked me—which suggested a lifetime of bad choices waiting for her.

"Is the plow guy coming?" I asked. It had snowed most of the time I was gone. "I could barely make it up the driveway."

"He comes when there's four inches, you know that," Nana Cole said. "You could have taken the Escalade. It'll drive through most anything."

I took the baby from Jan, and Emerald let out a tiny squeal. The sound that meant she was happy. *Yup,* I thought, *if I'm what makes her happy, the kid is doomed.*

The kitchen smelled like spaghetti sauce, and in one corner Riley was asleep in a dog bed I'd gotten him.

"Did you let Riley out?" I asked my grandmother who was standing by the stove stirring a giant pot, her cane in one hand.

"Oh yes, he did a nice big number two," Jan answered for her. She was the youngest of Nana Cole's friends and the most religious. She wore a big fuzzy sweater buttoned to her neck. Even for January she looked over-dressed.

"Thank you."

"Well, I should get going. I've got my own dinner to make," she said, standing up. She was single, a spinster, as my Nana Cole called her behind her back, so she might have been fishing for a dinner invite. It didn't come.

Jan was over by the coat hook next to the back door. I decided to sneak something in before she left. "Nana, have you heard from my mother?"

She gave me a sharp look and said, "She calls when she calls."

I glanced at Jan, trying to read her face. If my mother had called, I wouldn't be surprised if Nana Cole told her friends and not me. Jan looked a little cowed, but that might have been the tension in the room.

"I'll see you Friday, Emma," she said, then slipped out the door.

I put the baby in the car seat. I really wanted the seat to work, because if I did something crazy like go the bathroom and Nana Cole managed to knock the whole thing off the table, the baby would be fine. The seat was so sturdy, I was sure the whole house could fall down and Emerald would be just fine sitting in the seat amid the rubble.

I said I had to go upstairs and make a phone call, so I scurried out of the kitchen before Emerald could begin to fuss. On the way, I worried about my mother. A few days after New Year's, a Christmas a box had arrived with a Chicago postmark and no return address. Inside were some baby clothes that wouldn't fit Emerald for at least a year, a couple of toys she could have choked on, and a photograph of my mother and her boyfriend, David Hounsell. She wore a silky pale blue dress and held a small bouquet in her hands while he stood there, three-piece suit and slicked back hair looking like a poor man's Michael Douglas. On the back it said, 'Mr. and Mrs. David Hounsell, 12/21/2003."

They were standing in a living room. The furniture was

covered in a dusty pink fabric and the end tables were made of thick, whitewashed wood. I could see bits of the floor, which was tiled in terra cotta. They weren't in Chicago. They were somewhere in the Southwest. So why the Chicago postmark? Did they go to Chicago on their honeymoon? That didn't make sense. It was the middle of the winter. My mother hated winter.

She'd told me they weren't getting married because things were complicated. Now that they were married, were things uncomplicated? And how did they get uncomplicated?

In my bedroom, I got out my cell phone, scrolled through until I found Ham's name and hit send.

"Yeah."

"It's me. Henry."

"Yeah, I know. What's up?"

"I went to Three Friends and spoke to Melanie."

"What did you think?"

"There's a discrepancy."

"Okay. We like those."

"In her statement Roberta said she was walking from the toilet to the sink when she may have slipped on some water. But Melanie said the water was running in the sink. That suggests she made it to the sink and didn't fall until after she'd turned the water on."

"Good, that's exactly what we're looking for."

"Should I go talk to her and see what she says about it?"

"No. Don't go anywhere near her. The lawyers will ask the questions. They're going to want her answers under oath. And we don't want to give her time to come up with any plausible lies."

"Tomorrow I'm going to talk to one of the Three Friends employees and probably one of Roberta's friends."

"Careful when you talk to her friends. Try to let them do the talking. You don't want to say anything that will get back to Roberta."

"Okay." That was a bit nerve-racking. "Um... can I ask you a personal question?"

"About me? No. I'm none of your business."

"No, I mean about me. About my mother. She got married."

I told him all about the package and my theory that she was in the Southwest somewhere despite the Chicago postmark. This was really the only clue I had about my mother's movements other than my grandmother's Escalade being found just over the border in Indiana a week after my mother drove off in it.

"I've been keeping an eye out since you told me she ran off. Your stepfather's—"

"Please don't use that word."

"David's company, Hounsell Income Technologies, has filed for bankruptcy."

"How does that work? I mean, you said it's a hedge fund, which means people give you their money and you're supposed to make money for them and if you don't *they* lose money. Isn't that all there is to it?"

"Yes and no. Bankruptcy just means you owe more than you have, and you don't think you'll ever catch up."

"So, basically, he lost all his investors' money?"

"Possibly. Corporate bankruptcy can be a strategy. It does mean someone's going to get screwed."

"Do you have any idea where they are?"

"They could still be in California. Out in the desert, possibly San Diego. As nearly as I can tell he sold his boat right before he filed for bankruptcy. If that money went into his own pocket, they'll try to claw it back in the bankruptcy, but that could take years."

"Los Angeles is probably too expensive for them, so they might have rented someplace cheaper," I guessed.

"Your mother doesn't want you to know where she is. I doubt they rented an apartment. They're on the move."

"Like... on the run?"

"My guess would be that David screwed the wrong investor."

VILLAGE BOOKS OPENED at ten in the morning. I would have liked to have gotten there at exactly ten, but Nana Cole's physical therapy was at ten fifteen, and then she was tired afterward and then there was lunch which I had to make—a tuna fish sandwich for Nana Cole and a bottle of formula for the baby. By the time I was ready to eat my own sandwich, it was time to clean up and argue about the radio.

"I don't understand why I can't listen to the radio in my own home."

"You can. Just not when I'm in the room."

"You do remember that you're not paying room and board?"

"You do remember that you're not paying me for childcare or any of the other six million things I do for you?"

Okay, I didn't do six million things for her, but I did do a lot and she knew it. Quietly she said, "Your mother owes you for the childcare, not me."

"Whatever. I don't think it's too much to ask that I not have to listen to people like Dr. Laura and your friend Rush say horrible things."

"I happen to believe the same things they believe."

"Then you don't need to listen to them. You can be horrible all on your own."

I was probably being a little dramatic. Nana Cole wasn't exactly horrible. Yes, she *believed* horrible things, but she also didn't believe politics had much to do with real people. She thought her opinions were harmless. I wasn't as sure.

Bev and Barbara showed up at two. Normally, this was when I'd take a little nappy-poo. Instead, sleepy-eyed, I drove to Masons Bay and parked in front of Village Books. The bookstore had four connected rooms on one half of the first floor of what had once been a nice home. The conservancy where I'd once worked was located on the back side of the house.

A bell rang above my head when I entered the store. Even though it had changed hands twice since my last visit, the bookstore looked pretty much the same. There were books everywhere, including stacked on chairs and on the floor. As you walked in there was a counter with an antique cash register and a display of the bestsellers *The Da Vinci Code*, *To the Nines* and *The Five People You Meet in Heaven*. There were only two things that were different about the bookstore. One was a bookcase near the door that was entirely devoted to romance novels, with a sign that said, 'WE NOW CARRY ROMANCE!' surrounded by hearts. The other different thing was a stack of the book *Slander: Liberal Lies About the American Right* by Ann Coulter with a handprinted sign on top designating 50% OFF!

Penny Pelletier sat on a stool behind the counter. She was in her mid-thirties with peachy skin and thin colorless hair. Stereotypically, she wore glasses, and also wore an apron with many of the pins she sold attached. READERS DO IT BY THE BOOK stood out.

"Welcome to Village Books!" she said brightly.

"Hi, I'm Mo—Henry Milch. I'm an investigator working with Hamlet Gilbody..."

Okay, so I gave myself a promotion. I worked *for* him, not *with* him— but big deal, right?

"...we're looking into the fall Roberta LaCross took at Three Friends winery while you were working there."

"I remember. I already gave a statement to the insurance company."

"Yes. I read it. I just want to go over a few things."

"All right." She fidgeted on the stool. I was getting the strong feeling she didn't want to talk to me.

"I want confirm that you didn't wait on Roberta or anyone in her party."

"I did not."

"Do you remember about how long they were there?"

"A couple of hours."

"Do you have a sense of how much they drank? Did you notice a bottle on the table, maybe?"

"I had my own customers. I really don't know how much they drank."

Then I remembered Ham wanted me to get people talking and not say so much myself. Well, actually he wanted me to do that when I talked to Roberta's friends. Which made me ask, "Are you friends with Roberta?"

"I wasn't then. But she comes into the bookstore and we've gotten friendly. She's quite the character. She'll talk your ear off. And some of it's about books, so I don't really mind."

"Is that why you got uncomfortable when I asked about how she drank? Because you're friends?"

"I'm friends with Melanie, too. It's an awkward spot."

I decided to be more direct, "Do you think Roberta was overserved?"

"Maybe. Right before she went to the ladies' room her friends were teasing her about slurring her words."

"You remember that or she told you that?"

"Both."

I thanked her and was about to leave when I noticed the children's section. I walked over and stared at all the books for a moment. Without turning around I asked Penny, "When should you start reading to babies?"

"They say six months, but earlier is better."

Emerald was almost six months old, so, yeah, she needed books. It didn't take too long to figure out the earliest books were the ones that were fifteen or twenty thick cardboard pages long. Obviously, they were meant to stand up to a baby chewing on them, throwing them around, vomiting on them, and various other infant calamites.

I picked out *Good Night Moon, The Very Hungry Caterpillar* and *Brown Bear, Brown Bear What Do You See?* I also got *Where The Wild Things Are* and *Alexander and the Terrible, Horrible, No Good, Very Bad Day.* They were both too old for her, but *I* was interested. I especially wanted to read the Alexander one, because it basically sounded like my life. I also bought my grandmother a copy of *Stupid White Men* by Michael Moore.

Nana Cole would hate *Stupid White Men* and would never read it. But there was real joy in buying it for her. For one thing, it was on her credit card, so I was making her pay for it. For another, when she complained about it, I'd be able to say, "I'm sorry. But he's from Michigan. I thought you'd like it."

I giggled several times on the way home.

CHAPTER FOUR

The thing I hate about twelve-step meetings is that the whole point is to talk about your problems. Which makes no sense, since the whole point of taking drugs is to *not* even think about your problems. So why is the solution to taking drugs doing the thing that made you take them in the first place? See? It's completely illogical. Each time I went I felt like I'd have been better off just going to the movies.

Of course, I hadn't *exactly* stopped taking drugs. I'd stopped taking OxyContin. For one hundred and seventy-eight often difficult days. Edward—hot, sexy, Dr. Edward Stewart—was the one who gave me a prescription for 5 days of Ativan to get me through withdrawals.

Ativan and Valium are basically the same thing. Like the Chevy and Buicks of the pharmaceutical world. Anyway, I supplemented that prescription with some Valium I'd borrowed from Bev's purse—she was around a lot, so it was easy and irresistible. Apparently, she had epilepsy and had to take it occasionally. Relax. I always made sure to leave enough for her to get to the pharmacy for a refill.

Anyway, after a few weeks, I went back and begged Edward for another prescription. It took a very tense half hour

—he's a stubborn man, but he finally relented. I think it was my pretty eyes that did it. Or maybe because we were in the ER and he had to go save someone's life. Whichever.

He gave me enough for thirty days. Ninety pills. Ah, Edward. Seriously, it's hard not to adore a man who gives you drugs. Especially when he said he wouldn't and then he does anyway. Plus, he's gorgeous. Tall and auburn-haired, with blue eyes and razor-sharp cheekbones.

And... I left a standing order with Ronnie Sheck, our local drug dealer. He doesn't get Ativan or Valium often, but people do try to trade random prescription drugs for the more illicit ones. He showed me a shoebox full of pills ranging from Prozac to nitroglycerin. Very colorful.

That visit netted me another two hundred and some pills. Which seemed like an awful lot at the time but now I was nearly out, and I didn't want to go back to Edward. If he thought I'd stopped taking them, he might be willing to take another try at going out with me. It would be nice to have a sex life again. Especially one I might remember.

Basically, I had to find another doctor. It shouldn't be that hard. I'd gone to the Internet and looked up what Ativan was used for. Anxiety. I just needed to make an appointment, show up, explain my crippling anxiety in creative detail and get a prescription. And I *did* have anxiety. I was afraid if I stopped taking one drug (Ativan) I'd fall back into the habit of taking another drug (OxyContin). It was completely reasonable to alleviate that anxiety.

I know, I know, I shouldn't be taking any drugs at all while caring for a baby. But think about it. There have to be millions of women with anxiety and millions of women are taking care of babies. My bet is there's significant overlap. Drugged women raise babies all the time and nothing goes wrong. Or at least not a lot. So why can't I do it?

Which is not to say I wasn't careful. I didn't take anything at night, since I didn't want to sleep through Emerald's three o'clock feeding. I also didn't take anything in the morning, since that was usually the busiest time for Emerald. Feeding, changing, bouncing, chewing on random things—the whole deal. So mostly I took an Ativan when we had help in the afternoon. And then in the evenings, since Emerald usually slept from seven to ten. See, I've thought this through.

Anyhoo, I decided to go to that Thursday night LGBT NA meeting Opal mentioned. Solely out of curiosity, you understand. And it might be nice to be in a roomful of queer people. Even if they were fucked up.

The meeting was held in the pole barn behind Cheswick Community Church. The intersection of church, drug stuff and gay stuff made me anxious enough to wish I'd taken an Ativan. And then there was the whole accepting of a higher power thing the twelve-steppers wanted you to do. That was enough to make me want an Oxy. Real bad.

I don't believe in God, so that leaves me short a higher power. They did say I could choose anything as my higher power. They suggested the universe, but I was a little cool on that idea. If God was responsible for a lot of really shitty things, then so was the universe. At that moment, I was leaning toward Cher as my higher power. For one thing she was old and at least tried to do good things and for another "Believe" was kind of spiritual, right?

So there I was at the pole barn behind the church. Again. I arrived late, on purpose. They had fellowship before and after and I really hated that. Seriously, a bunch of addicts standing around drinking coffee, eating cookies, and smoking didn't do much for me. I mean, really. Caffeine, sugar and nicotine. Yeah, we've given up our addictions. Ha!

I slipped into an empty seat and realized that I knew the guy who was talking. His name was Richard. The last time I saw him was in the emergency room and he was a toxic yellow.

"... it was hard, but I've been clean for six months and have finally been allowed onto the transplant list. About twenty percent of people on the list die while waiting, so that six months didn't help my chances. But I should be grateful. At least now I have a chance."

The little group applauded. Limply, I joined in. I looked around the group of about twelve. The only other person I knew was Todd Turley—wait, that's not his name. He works at the Turley HIV clinic. It's just Todd or Toddy maybe. No idea about his last name. Todd was in his thirties, very tall and thin, with a prominent Adam's apple. Honestly, he looked like a sexy Icahbod Crane. I know that sounds impossible, but it's true.

Aside from Todd and Richard there were only two other guys. Both wore flannel and looked like the rednecks I avoided at the grocery store. Maybe they were in the wrong meeting. The women ran the gamut from bull dyke to super femme. Honestly, sometimes I wished people would wear name tags that made things clearer. Todd, gay. Elisa, bisexual. Wanda, lesbian. Bill, lost. That would be so helpful.

Of course, the guy named Bill spoke up and answered my question. He spent the rest of the meeting complaining about how his wife kept claiming his drug use (meth) was the reason he was sleeping with men. It wasn't and he could prove it. He'd been sober for nearly a year and had had sex with eight different guys (which suggested maybe I shouldn't avoid the redneck types so carefully). Yes, he missed having sex while he was high, but he'd been having sex with his wife while high and he missed that, too.

Bill's talk of sex was getting boring, so I snuck looks at Todd. I liked his blond hair, which was much darker underneath, sun bleached even in the depths of winter. His eyes were pale blue. And that Adam's apple. Was he knobby like that all over?

And then the meeting was done. Thank god. I decided to make a quick exit—right after I snagged a cookie off the refreshment table. And boom, there was Todd.

"Hi, I remember you."

"Mooch."

"No—Henry, right?"

"Yeah."

"Do you have a sponsor yet?"

"Oh, you know, I've only been a few times. Not sure if I'm going to keep coming."

"What's your drug of choice?"

"I had a little problem with Oxy but it's over. Done. In the past. I really don't need all this."

"When you're ready, I'd be willing to be your sponsor."

"Okay, um, sure. I'll remember that."

"And don't worry. I'm not trying to thirteenth-step you."

"Wait. I thought there are only twelve steps?" Had they added a step? That was not good news.

"The thirteenth step is having sex with other people in the program."

Oh. Well, if there was no sex I definitely didn't want him to be my sponsor. Brilliantly, I said, "Yeah. Okay. Bye."

When I got home, I took an Ativan. It would wear off by the time Emerald woke up and needed to be fed. I hoped.

THE NEXT MORNING, we had a visit with the pediatrician at nine-thirty. Our pediatrician was a woman named Tamara Sampson who liked to be called Dr. Tammy. She'd taken over Dr. Blinski's office, most of the first floor of an old River Rock house on the edge of Masons Bay. She had not taken over his practice, that had gone to a medical group in Bellflower. You'd be surprised by how much time people devoted to complaining about driving twenty-five minutes to see a doctor rather than five.

Anyway, despite its being a five-minute drive from my Nana Cole's farm, we were twenty minutes early, mainly because I over-estimated how long it would take to get a baby and a slightly disabled senior citizen into a Cadillac SUV. I was better at attaching the safety belt to the car seat than I gave myself credit for and giving my grandmother a boost into the passenger seat that she didn't want was quicker when I simply ignored her protests.

In the waiting room, I said, "You should have brought that Michael Moore book to read."

"You think you're funny, but you're not."

I was funny but decided not to argue with her. Instead, I read through the parts of the Three Friends file I hadn't looked at yet. Roberta had gone to the winery with two friends, Zoey Calder and Patty Gauthier. Each statement gave their addresses, phone numbers and where they worked, so I knew how to find them. Zoey's statement made reference to how much fun Roberta was. It was apparently Patty's fiftieth birthday that day, which was why they were there in the first place. She claimed they heard their friend screaming, but that Melanie had gotten to the ladies' room first and wouldn't let them in. She and Patty hovered near the door calling out encouragement until the ambulance got there. Patty's statement was similar, though she complained that after the ambulance left Melanie brought their bill and Patty, the birthday girl, ended up paying it. The statement didn't say whether she'd used cash or credit.

Finally, it was time for us to go in. The nurse led us back to the exam room. The room where Dr. Blinski was killed. The room where I fell on top of his corpse. It had been redecorated, of course. Now it was pink and blue with teddy bear wallpaper. Still, being there was just a tad creepy.

The nurse took Emerald's vitals: her pulse by holding two fingers on her bicep, her temperature by aiming a contraption into her ear, blood pressure with a tiny cuff on her thigh. Finally, the nurse sat Emerald up and then left her there for a moment. She wobbled, then the nurse picked her up and was about to give her to my grandmother when I reached out and took her.

"Are you here for anything specific or just a routine check?" she asked my grandmother.

"Routine," I answered.

"Okay then. The doctor will be in shortly." Still not to me. Now I knew what women felt like at a car dealership.

After the door shut, Nana Cole said, "Don't ask a lot of questions."

"Why not? We're not paying by the question. We might as well get our money's worth."

"I've done this before, you know. I can answer any questions you have."

"You haven't done it recently. Things change."

"Change isn't always better. Sometimes it's just change."

The doctor came in. She was in her early forties with gray hair that curled like a Brillo pad. The door wasn't closed behind her before she began to baby-talk at Emerald. I set the baby on the exam table in a sitting position. She maintained it for longer than she had with the nurse.

"Very good," Dr. Tammy said. She picked up the baby and lay her on her stomach. We waited until Emerald had wiggled around and finally rolled over. I nearly said, 'Good girl.' She been rolling over for several weeks, and given Dr. Tammy's previous questions I knew it was something she was supposed to be doing.

"Are you feeding her solids?"

"We should have started months ago," Nana Cole said. "He wouldn't let me."

I glared at her. She was trying to rat me out to the doctor.

"Well, she's got good head and neck control, and she's almost sitting on her own." She'd picked the baby up and put her back in a sitting position, bracing her back with one hand. "Does she seem interested in your food?"

I had no idea. Typically, I fed them first and they were

usually in the living room while I ate. I gave my grandmother a questioning look.

"Does that really matter?" she asked. "She's supposed to eat when she's supposed to eat."

The doctor explained, "When I was a child, doctors recommended keeping babies on a strict schedule, they didn't believe in babies doing things early or late. I believe you let the baby lead. Try putting her in the high chair and giving her some rice cereal or mashed banana. If she spits it out, don't force it. Try again in a week. Or even a few days. Her weight is in the ninety-fifth percentile. There's no reason to force food."

"Great. We'll do that."

It's not that I was in a rush for Emerald to grow up, it's just that I was in a rush for her to grow up. For one thing, diapers. For another, someday I'd need more help with my grandmother. She might be useful by the time she's eight. Maybe even seven.

Wait, what was I thinking? I wasn't hanging around here for eight years. I was going back to Los Angeles. I was going back *soon*. Maybe I'd just bring Emerald with me? Leave my grandmother to fend for herself? Okay that was all really complicated. There were a lot of details to work out. I was going to have to think it through. Another time.

Before the visit ended, Dr. Tammy asked, "Have you heard anything from Emerald's mommy?"

"She and Emerald's daddy have gotten married, and they'll be setting up house soon."

"What? When did you—" I shut up. There was a lie afoot here, I just wasn't sure who was being lied to, me or the doctor.

"Well, I hope they set up nearby. I'd love to watch Emerald grow up. She looks great. I'll see you back in about a month. Stop at the desk and make an appointment on your way out. If it turns out, if Mommy comes back and you don't need it you can go ahead and cancel."

The door shut and I glared at my grandmother, "Did you talk to my mother and not tell me?"

"Why are you asking me that?"

"They'll be setting up house soon?"

"That's what people do after they get married, isn't it?"

"You know she doesn't follow those kinds of rules. People don't usually get married *after* they have the baby, people don't usually have a baby when they've got a twenty-four-year-old son, and people don't usually disappear and abandon their kids. Do they?"

She sighed and said, "I'm going to wait in the car."

As she wobbled out of the exam room I called after her, "Don't you dare try to get in all by yourself."

We hadn't locked the car. It was Masons Bay, after all. Still, I had the keys in my pocket. I took them out, aimed the fob at the front of the building, and pressed LOCK. Hopefully, that would do it.

I secured the baby in her carrier and went out to the front desk. Over Emerald's screams, I asked that they send an invoice for the visit then made an appointment for the next visit in a month. I walked out of the building half expecting to see my grandmother spread out across the sidewalk. But she was leaning on her cane next to the passenger door looking like she wanted to spit on me.

"You locked the doors."

"I did. Let me get the baby settled and I'll help you in." I unlocked the doors with the fob. As I reached for the back door, Nana Cole opened hers and made to scramble in. I set the baby carrier down in a snowbank and got behind her in case she fell. Luckily, she didn't.

When she got into her seat, she saw me there and said, "Get off me." I decided to interpret that as 'Thank you.'

I got the baby situated in the back seat, climbed in behind the wheel, then drove three blocks and parked again in front of Fudge You!

"What are you doing?" Nana Cole asked.

"I need to go into the fudge store for a minute or two."

"No, you're not giving the baby fudge. You heard the doctor, rice cereal or mushed up fruit."

"That's not why—I need to talk to someone who works there. Okay?"

"Oh. Fine." Before I got the door fully open, she added, "Get me half a pound of chocolate pecan." She opened her purse and dug around for her wallet. She gave me a five and I got out of the SUV.

Inside, Fudge You! was a narrow storefront with glass cases on one side and two marble-topped tables in the center. I knew from previous visits that the fudge was made on the marble and that somehow made it special. Don't ask me how.

Behind the cases, dressed in a red-and-white smock, was an awkward looking girl a few years older than me. She wasn't who I was looking for, that was clear.

"Hi, I'm looking for Zoey Calder. Do you know when she'll be here?"

"I'm Zoey."

"Oh, okay. Are there two Zoeys?"

"I don't think so. I mean, maybe somewhere there's another one. Who are you?"

"I'm Mooch Milch. I'm working for—"

"I'm sorry, what did you say your name was? Moo-moo?"

I really needed to give up on that nickname. "Henry. Henry Milch. I'm working for an agency investigating the fall Roberta LaCross took at Three Friends winery. You were with her that day?"

"Yeah, I was."

"You and Roberta are friends?"

"We are. Yeah."

I reminded myself to ask open-ended questions. "How did you become friends?"

"You think it's weird, don't you? Because Bobbie's older.

We play trivia together at Main Street Café. We're on a team together called the Boomers. Most of the team are baby boomers. Except me and Bobbie, I'm a millennial and she's... gosh what comes before boomers?"

"Got me," I said, trying to smile. "And how do you know Patty Gauthier?"

"Trivia. She's an actual boomer."

"So, what is Roberta like?"

That got me a frown. "It's so weird that you keep calling her Roberta. She's Bobbie. Everyone calls her Bobbie. Everyone who knows her. I mean, she's in Main Street Café most nights."

"I'm from Los Angeles."

"I guess that explains the outfit."

I almost asked what was wrong with my outfit. I was wearing my cheap blue puffer jacket, rubberized winter boots, lavender leg warmers (yes, I know no one has worn leg warmers since the year I was born, but I found them at a thrift shop, and they *are* warm), my lime green sweater—which I'd spot cleaned, and a black-and-white piano key scarf.

"Do you play the piano?"

"No, I just thought it was a cool scarf." I'd been asked that question a half dozen times, I was going to have to find another scarf or start piano lessons.

"What is Rob... Bobbie like?"

"Bobbie is the *best*. Such a character. So much fun to be with! The stories she tells. She's had a really incredible life. I mean, yeah, she repeats her stories a lot and that annoys some people, but the stories don't always turn out the same, so they never annoy me. I mean, she's had a hard life. Those ex-husbands, I'd feel sorry for her if she wasn't so funny all the time, you know?"

"Tell me what happened the day you went to Three Friends. It was Patty Gauthier's fiftieth birthday?"

"It was. There were supposed to be a lot more of us. But,

well... Patty is someone who speaks her mind. I think it's refreshing, but some people think it's just being a bitch. Actually, it was embarrassing that almost no one came. Patty didn't deserve that."

"Did you guys get drunk?"

"I didn't."

"Did Bobbie?"

"Bobbie's a lightweight."

"You said she's in Main Street Café most nights. She's not drinking?"

"Well, I mean, she is... Honestly, I think someone gives her a ride home most of the time."

"Right before she fell, was Bobbie slurring her words?"

"Oh, I mean, not really."

"Not really?"

She smiled and said, "I don't really remember what I'm supposed to say."

"You're supposed to tell me the truth."

"Well... yeah."

"You and Patty were teasing Bobbie about slurring her words?"

"That makes us sound awful. I guess, yeah. That's true but it wasn't like serious. It was just a joke."

"She must have been slurring her words if you teased her about it."

"It's better for Bobbie if I say she was slurring her words, isn't it?"

"Would you lie to me so Bobbie wins her lawsuit?"

"Oh my god, no. I'm not like that. What she said was, 'I have to go to the bassroom.' Like it's a room for fish."

I decided to switch tracks. "Did you go into the bathroom after Rob... Bobbie fell?"

"I stood outside the door. There was water on the floor."

"Was the faucet running?"

"I don't know. Why would that matter?"

"What else do you remember from that afternoon?"

"We were having fun. Bobbie was on. You know, cracking jokes, telling stories. Back then, she had an apartment on Crystal Lake. This dentist owned the place, like three apartments right on the water. Bobbie's faced away from the water, which is why she could afford it at all. The two in the front were weekend rentals all summer. Anyway, she was telling stories about the tourists and how crazy some of them are. And the bugs."

"The bugs?"

"There's a lot of bugs out that way. Mosquitos, gnats, moths, fireflies, all that. The tourists would spray themselves with all sorts of chemicals, but Bobbie didn't care. She just let the bugs bite, you know?"

Honestly, one of the best things about winter in Michigan was no bugs.

CHAPTER FIVE

That afternoon, it was snowing when Dorothy showed up to help. After a little bit of a chat about the baby, I got into my car and drove up M-22 to a home just above Masons Bay. Patty Gauthier had a large house on the west side of M-22, which meant that she had a small slip of land right on the water. Her house was two stories with faded wood shingles. There was a two-car garage with an apartment above it. There was so much house, I couldn't see the water when I pulled the Metro into her paved driveway.

Each side of the driveway had a tall snowbank, and there was a mountain of snow that had been plowed up next to the garage. A woman in her early fifties with a long braid of gray hair flopping around was in front of the garage door using a snow shovel to scrape ice off the black top. She wore a tall pair of UGGS and a coat that looked like it had once been a blanket. Patty Gauthier.

Telling her who I was and what I was doing there earned me an unhappy look.

"I don't want to talk about Bobbie."

"Okay, that's not really going to help her case."

"Who said I wanted to help her case?"

"Your original statement supported what Patty said. Did she tell you what to say?"

"I plead the fifth."

"Um, you know it's just a civil case. Nothing's going to happen to you if you admit to telling a little white lie."

I had no idea if that was true, but then I guess she did because she said, "Um. Bill Clinton was impeached for committing perjury in a civil case. So... I plead the fifth."

"When did you and Bobbie stop being friends? You can answer that because it's not part of your statement."

She chewed on that for a moment, and said, "Last Spring. May, beginning of June. Yeah. It was June definitely."

"What happened? I got the impression you were good friends."

"She doesn't have friends; she has people she uses." I checked her ears to see if smoke was coming out. "She broke her arm. That's what happened. Stupidly, I told her she could stay with me while she got better. I've got the room, or at least thought I did. When it happened, she needed to stay as still as she possible, so I took her in. Cooked for her, took care of her. After eight weeks she could do a lot more on her own, so I asked when she was going home. Come to find out, without telling me, she'd had some guys move her out of her apartment and put her things in storage. She was saving six hundred dollars a month living with me."

"So, you threw her out?"

"Not for another eight months. It was the holidays. I couldn't throw her out at Thanksgiving. Or Christmas. And then it was the dead of winter. And then she broke her wrist."

"How did she do that?"

"I'd given her the master bedroom, my bedroom. It's on the first floor and there's an ensuite. I moved to the apartment above the garage. When I worked up the courage to tell her to get out, she tripped while walking across her—*my* bedroom. Apparently, she fell into the door and broke it. It took until

June to get her out of here. She mooched off me for almost a year."

I cringed a little at the way she'd used the word mooch. I had the feeling she wanted me to. I waited. Finally, she said, "After I threw her out, she went around telling people I'd treated her badly while she was recovering. Both times. That I wouldn't hang out with her and play cards, that I wouldn't cook anything she liked, that I just left her lying there week after week which wasn't fair at all. I bought a new TV and DVD player for the bedroom, and I don't even watch TV."

"Was she drunk at your birthday lunch?"

She gave me a look that said she knew exactly what I was doing. After a moment, she answered. "No. She was *not* drunk. And she was *not* overserved. And I didn't say she was in my statement."

"Were you and Zoey teasing her about slurring her words?"

"That wasn't alcohol. You can't be much of a private investigator if you haven't figured out she was on drugs most of the time."

Okay, that was harsh. "Um... well... I only got the case a few days ago."

"Well, you didn't hear that from me. I'm not officially saying anything against her. There's no telling what she'll do."

"Do you know what she was taking?"

"Some kind of antianxiety medication. Atta-boy?"

"Ativan?" I supplied. This was a little uncomfortable. Was I slurring my words? Did people notice?

"Yeah. That's it. When she was staying with me, I saw that she had a giant bottle of it."

"Do you know where she got it?"

Well, it was a relevant question, don't you think?

"From a doctor. It was prescription."

"Oh, yeah. That makes sense. Um... Is there anything else you left out of your statement?"

The flood gates were open, she said, "It was a mosquito bite."

"What?"

"On her shin. She picked at it until it bled. She went into the ladies' room to wash it off. She put her foot into the sink. That's why she fell."

"Okay, wait? An old lady put her foot in the sink?"

"She was very flexible. And proud of it. All you have to do is say the word yoga and she'll spend an hour telling you she's practically a yogi."

"What about her shoe? No one mentioned that she wasn't wearing her shoe? I mean, she did take her shoe off, right?"

"It was August. She had on this kind of loose sandal. I think they're called slides. Way too young for her but... It probably didn't strike anyone as odd that her sandal came off. I mean, she was on the floor. Why wouldn't it?"

"It would be really helpful if you could make a new statement."

I was making an assumption, but it seemed logical that it would be. She was shaking her head even before I got the whole sentence out.

"Why not? She obviously treated you badly and it's not fair that the winery might have to pay her." I waited. She didn't say anything, so I asked. "Are you afraid of her?"

"Well, she did kill a man."

"Would you like to tell me about that?"

"No. I wouldn't. It's time for you to go."

On the way home, I thought about what to do next. Dorothy wouldn't be at the house for another two hours. I could slip upstairs and take a nap like I usually did in the afternoon. But then, well, I was kind of excited. There was no way Bobbie's fall was the fault of the winery. It wasn't about some fragile old lady they'd gotten drunk who then slipped on their wet bathroom floor. It was about an addict who went into the ladies' room and did something stupid. She didn't stand a chance. I'd just finished my first job, and I'd done really, really well.

I stopped at Cuppa Mud in Masons Bay. The little coffee shop had a cement floor painted gray, walls painted white, and a counter made of raw wood. There were a lot of plants.

In fact, more plants than people. There were only three people there. I got a latte and sat in a corner. I took out my cell phone and called Hamlet.

"Hello," he whispered. There was a lot of ambient noise in the background."

"Hey. Where are you?"

"I'm in a park. Do we need to talk now?"

"Real quickly then... Bobbie LaCross is a drug addict who went into the ladies' room at Three Friends, stuck her foot in the sink to rinse off a mosquito bite, and lost her balance. The whole thing was her own fault."

"Good job," he said. I almost asked him to repeat that, but I'd heard it just fine. "Make some notes and email them to me. I'll talk with the client tomorrow. And send me an invoice."

I wanted to extend the conversation, hopefully he'd compliment me another three or four times, but, in a cloud of fake lavender fur, Opal sat down across from me. Her hair was now cobalt blue with white smudges here and there. She noticed me looking at them and said, "They're supposed to be stars. If you say one word, I'll break your arm."

Interesting choice of words.

I needed to ask Ham how much he was paying me, but he said he had to go, which might have had something to do with his being in a park in the middle of winter, so I agreed and hung up.

"What are you doing here?"

"Pastiche is practically across the street. I saw you walk in, so I decided it was break time. I mean, it's the dead of winter, I'm not even sure why we're open. So? Was he there?"

"Was who where?"

"Denny. Was he at the meeting?"

"Why do you think I went to the meeting? Did someone tell you I was there?"

"I knew you'd be curious. That's why I told you about the Thursday meeting. You went, didn't you?"

I was so tempted to say no, but instead I said, "Your friend Richard was there. Boy, does he look bad."

"We're not friends."

"You *were* friends."

"Until he stole half the reward money."

"He what?"

"You heard me. I had to put half the money up myself."

"You told me you put in five hundred."

"You're not the only one who can lie."

Whoa, I caught her in a lie and she called *me* out as a liar. That takes nerve. Mad respect, though. I mean, it made me hate her guts, but I was still impressed.

"Was Denny at the meeting?"

"No, he wasn't. And why do you care so much—oh, crap. Your thing for Carl, you want to sabotage their relationship by telling him Denny doesn't go to meetings."

Opal immediately flushed, her red cheeks, blue hair and white smudges making her look very patriotic—though it would have been a better look in July.

"I have to go. Thanks, but no thanks for the info."

When I got home there was still time for a short nap. I checked in the kitchen, gave Emerald a tickle in her high chair —she began to fuss. I let Riley back in and scolded my grandmother for trying to keep him outside. It was a warm day but still barely in the twenties.

"You act like I'm a monster. If you're worried about your dog build him a doghouse." Then she said to Dorothy, who was at the stove sterilizing bottles despite being told to use the dishwasher repeatedly, "He sleeps with the mangy thing."

"Oh yeah, all my grandkids do. It's the way they are."

"I don't know what we did wrong."

Meanwhile, as the baby began to cry, I gave Riley fresh water and a big bowl of kibble. "I'm going to take a nap. If you let Riley out, let him back in."

Then I went upstairs, scurrying away from Emerald's screams, and took an Ativan.

CHAPTER SIX

When I woke up it was dark. I glanced at the clock, seven. Why was it seven? Distantly, I heard a small voice saying, "Help. Please help..." My Nana Cole.

I got out of bed and padded down the stairs to the first floor. In the kitchen, my grandmother was on the floor. Emerald was happily crawling around next to her.

When Nana Cole saw me, she said, "Thank God. I've been calling for forever."

"Why didn't you wake me up when Dorothy left?"

"We called up the stairs and you wouldn't wake up."

Okay, so maybe I took two Ativan. I was having trouble remembering.

"Dorothy just left?"

"She had things to do. She has a life."

"Everyone living has a life." I picked up the baby and strapped her into the car seat. She seemed to be smirking, as though she'd engineered this whole situation.

"How did you end up on the floor?"

"I fell. Is it that hard to figure out?"

"Were you holding the baby when you fell?"

I was giving Emerald a subtle exam, gently squeezing her limbs to see if she cried, touching her head to make sure it hadn't been flattened on one side.

"I didn't let go of her and she didn't hit the ground."

"You know you're not supposed to take her out of the car seat when you're alone."

"She was getting fussy. And why aren't you asking me if *I'm* hurt?"

She was still on the floor, so I'd assumed she was. She was also talking, bitching, making excuses for herself. So I knew she couldn't be hurt badly.

"Have you tried to get up?"

"No, I've been enjoying my time on the floor. Of course, I've tried to get up. I've been trying for the last half an hour."

"Do you want me to call an ambulance?"

"Don't be stupid. Just help me up."

I bent down and slipped my hands under her arms to pick her up the way I would Emerald. She was saying, "Not like that. Stop—" Too late, I'd lifted her off the floor. She really was a lot more fragile than she looked. She screamed a little, but I got her to her feet.

"Chair... chair..."

I pulled out a dining chair and set her in it.

"Ah... ah... oh sweet Jesus..."

"I'll get your coat and purse, and we can go after I check to see if the baby needs to be changed."

"Go where?"

"To the emergency room," I said, though it seemed obvious to me.

"No. Help me into my chair." She meant the one in the living room, not the one she was sitting in.

"You might have broken your hip. We're going to the ER."

"Just get me to my chair and I'll be fine by tomorrow."

"Get there yourself," I said, to prove a point.

Pressing down on the table, she tried to lift herself out of the chair. She struggled mightily to not make a peep as she did. I gave Emerald the sniff test. She was fine for now. The diaper bag (vintage Winnie the Pooh from the '60s and used for my mother and later me) sat near the front door; I was pretty sure it hadn't been touched and had everything we'd need. My grandmother was still trying to get out of the chair. I went down the hall and took her coat off the coatrack and brought it back to her.

"No."

"Okay. I'll warm up the car. If you're not in the living room by the time I come back we're going."

I walked out the back door, wondering if I should just call an ambulance. I could get her to the hospital if she cooperated, but it didn't seem like she was going to do that. And it would be nice if she was someone else's problem, if only for the time it took to get to the hospital.

Riley followed me out the back door. He'd like to go to the hospital. He'd like to go anywhere. I started the car and then threw down some more rock salt onto the back steps. Back inside, Nana Cole was exactly where she'd been when I walked outside. I braced myself for more negativity, but then she said, "I couldn't get the coat on."

I'd won. Not as satisfying as winning the lottery but still a victory. I had to take what I could get. I grabbed her coat, which was possibly older than I was. Then lifted her off the chair again.

"Okay, you're going to need to hold onto me. Grab my sweater." I thought that was magnanimous since she'd likely stretch it out. And I really did love that sweater. Seriously. It was lime, for god's sake.

Anyway, while she was clinging to me, I put the coat behind her then had her slip her arms in one at a time. Then, without asking, since I knew that would be a bad idea, I bent down and picked her up in a fireman's carry. I learned that watching *Baywatch*. I knew there was a reason to watch that show other than guys in bathing suits—though the male to female ratio on the show was not at all... Okay, fine, we'll talk about that later.

"Put me down! Put me down now!"

I ignored her. Putting her down only meant we'd be stuck wherever I put her down. Still, she kept demanding to be put down until I got to the SUV, opened passenger door, and plunked her onto the seat. Not too gently.

"FUCK!" she roared.

Hmmm, this might be bad. I mean, I'd never heard her swear like that. I ran back to house, collected the baby in her car seat, the diaper bag, forced Riley into the house against his will, and then went back to the Escalade. Once I got Emerald strapped in, we were off.

At the entrance to the ER at the recently renamed HealthWeb Hospital (formerly Midland Hospital, formerly Morley Medical Center, formerly St. Anne's), I jumped out of the car, grabbed the baby and hurried in. I told the receptionist, "My grandmother is in the car, she's taken a bad fall and is in a lot of pain. I need help getting her inside."

It seemed like forever, but was probably a whole two minutes, before an orderly, dressed entirely in scrubs, came out with a wheelchair.

"Your grandmother can sit, right? She's not lying in the back seat, is she?"

"No, she's sitting."

"Great," he said as he pushed through the automatic doors.

Behind him I said, "It's the Escalade." Not that there were many other choices. I mean, I'd parked right in front, and I could see my grandmother wincing at us through the passenger window.

Once the orderly had gotten Nana Cole into the wheelchair, she moaned loudly but managed not to swear again. He wheeled her directly into the emergency room. He took us to an exam... bay? Is that what they're called when there's no actual room just a bunch of spaces defined by thin curtains? I should know, I'd been there enough... But you know, no one gives you a tour. Anyway, we went right in. Like the pretty people at an LA club.

There was a chair, so I sat down and took Emerald out of the car seat so she wouldn't fuss. I got her onto my lap, and she immediately started pulling on my sweater—determined to complete the misshaping Nana Cole had started. Once the orderly wrangled Nana Cole onto the exam table, he said, "The nurse will be here in a minute."

"Thanks for your help," I said, as my sister tried to put her hand into my mouth.

As soon as he left, Nana Cole said, "He wasn't gentle."

"Do you want to leave?"

She glared at me for a moment before saying, "I don't *want* anything. I'm just telling you."

While we waited, Emerald and I stared at each other. Frequently, she had a dubious look on her face. I know babies at her age can't form sophisticated thoughts, but I could see that ideas were floating around, trying to connect, and I expected that her first full sentence would be 'What the fuck?'

Then Edward walked in. I was speechless for a moment. I often was with him. He probably thought I was an idiot. And in that moment, I probably was.

"Hello." He looked at the baby and said, "So, this is the result of your visit last fall, I assume?"

"This is Emerald."

"Hello, Emerald."

She smiled flirtatiously. Clearly, we were related.

Turning to my grandmother, he asked, "Now, what happened to you?"

Before she could answer, I said, "She took a fall with the baby, even though I told her—"

"I had an accident," she interrupted. "The kind people have. And the nurse hasn't been in yet. You're early."

"It's all right. I remember how to do vitals." He walked over to her and began taking them. He held her wrist for a half a minute then said, "You fell while holding the baby. Did the baby hit her head?"

"No," I said. "I don't think so."

"I was careful. I didn't drop her."

He stopped and looked the baby over quickly. That meant he was very close to me. His smelled amazing. I was tempted to toss the baby aside and just grab him.

Then, to Nana Cole he said, "You did a good job. Though you may have made things worse for yourself."

My mood changed quickly. Was she going to come out of this a hero? She was explicitly told not to—I would have made that point, but Edward was checking her heart with his stethoscope. He looked like he was having trouble finding it.

Apparently he did though, because he announced he was going to exam her hips. "Did you fall on one side? Or did you fall flat on your back?"

"More on the left."

Emerald maintained her balance by pulling on my hair. I really needed to give her a toy or something. Unfortunately, the diaper bag was on the other side of the exam table.

To me, Edward said, "I thought your mother was just visiting. When do she and the baby go back to California?"

"I guess you've missed the gossip. She disappeared."

Nana Cole squeaked. He'd found her left hip.

"Sorry," he said. Then, "Your mother disappeared? You don't think something horrible..."

"Nothing happened to her," my grandmother said. "She sent a Christmas card."

"Do you know when she's coming back?"

"Not a clue."

"She married Emerald's father."

Awkwardly, Edward said, "Well, that's something. Can you lift your leg?"

As my grandmother grimaced, I said, "Is it something, though? I can't work out if it's better to be abandoned by two parents or just one."

Oh my god, I could hear the anger in my voice. Getting angry in front of the sexy doctor who occasionally gave me pills was a terrible idea. I shut up.

"Okay, I'm going to send you for X-rays. Sorry we don't have a portable machine. Too small a hospital."

He nodded at both of us and then left. I scooted out after him, baby bouncing in my arms. "Edward."

Turning back to me he asked, "Did I forget something?"

"I just, um, I don't mean to sound so pissed off."

"Sounds like your mom is being irresponsible. It's okay to be pissed about that."

"Oh. Okay. Yeah, I'm pissed."

We kind of gaped at each other for a moment. Then he spoiled the moment by asking, "The situation isn't... How are you doing with the pills?"

"Well, I could use another prescription, if you're so inclined."

Emerald took that moment to wallop me in the face with one hand. Really? She couldn't possibly understand—

"Not what I meant," Edward said, then he whispered, "Oxy?"

"I haven't had any of that for a hundred and eighty days. Eighty-one? Eighty-two? Something like that."

"Good. Good for you. There's a chip for that, isn't there?"

"I have no idea."

"Well..."

He looked like he was going to walk away from me, so I blurted out, "Rather than a chip... How many days before we can try having another date?"

"I'm not really supposed to date patients."

"I'm not a patient. My grandmother is."

"You've been my patient. Repeatedly."

"Um... Isn't that a problem? This is the only hospital in like two hundred miles. Basically, everyone is your patient."

"That's occurred to me."

He paused and then after a moment said, "Let me think about it. I need to go order your grandmother's X-ray."

When I was back inside Nana Cole's bay, curtain-room, whatever, I put Emerald back into her car seat which resulted in her starting to cry. I looked up and Nana Cole was glowering at me in a way that made me say, "None of this is my fault."

Had she heard my conversation with Edward? She might have. There was basically a threadbare piece of cloth hanging between us. Crap. I mean, not crap. Screw her. She had to know I was gay. I mean, I did tell her, and I haven't exactly been hiding it. She knew. Right?

I dug Emerald's plastic keys out of the diaper bag, and waved them in front of her. She paused the sobbing, took them, threw them on the floor, then began crying again. I picked them up, they'd need to be washed, and while I was down there, I realized she needed to be changed.

"I'm going to go change the baby," I told my grandmother as I grabbed the car seat and the diaper bag.

In the men's room, as I was washing the keys with a little soap—not a lot, I didn't want her swallowing a lot of soap any more than I wanted her swallowing whatever lived on a hospital floor—while I was doing that I thought, *What the fuck am I doing here?*

Two years before, well, maybe eighteen months. During pride month 2002, I went out to West Hollywood every night for eleven days straight and did not pay a single door cover, did not pay for a single cocktail or any of the various and sundry pills I popped into my mouth. Now, I know that's not Nobel Peace Prize-worthy, but it *is* an accomplishment. One that I'm rather proud of. One that I'm afraid I might never repeat if I don't get back to Los Angeles soon. Young gay men have a shelf life and I could feel my expiration date approaching. But instead of enjoying my moment, I was holding a dirty disposable diaper in my hand with my nasty, broken grandmother in the other room.

It was wrong. All wrong.

CHAPTER SEVEN

Nana Cole's hip was not broken. She did have significant arthritis in her spine and pelvis, and she'd likely compressed a nerve in the fall—we'd have to do an MRI to be sure and if she didn't improve in a few days that's what we'd do.

Oh, goody.

She was given steroids, muscle relaxants and Tylenol. I think Edward might have given her some Oxy if he didn't think I was likely to steal it. But I wouldn't have stolen it. I'm almost certain.

When we got home, I settled Nana Cole on the sofa in the living room, where she spent the weekend and planned to stay until further notice. Of course, I tried to call my mother. Repeatedly. Her mother had injured herself. She'd want to know that, wouldn't she? She didn't answer. She never answered, it wasn't the first time I called and her mailbox had been full since early December.

Interestingly, my cell phone was still working. Since I was on my mother's plan, that meant she was paying the bill. And that she was receiving the bill. She'd let Verizon know where she was, but not me.

Right before Thanksgiving, I'd gone to the Verizon store

and attempted to get some information. I explained that my mother had lost her phone and she wanted me to see if they could find it for her. Could they check its location? The sales guy explained that they couldn't give out that information without a court order.

"You mean, you can't even tell me that when I'm standing right here?"

"Why would you need me to tell you that?"

Then he offered to give us an upgrade on my mother's phone. I declined and tried a different approach. "We haven't gotten our bill this month. Could I verify the address on the account?"

He looked at the screen and said, "Go ahead."

"What address do you have?"

"What address should we have?"

"I don't know what address my mother gave you."

"I can't tell *you* the address on the account. You can tell *me* what the address should be, and I can tell you if it's correct. If it's not correct your mother will have to change it herself."

"So, you think my mother doesn't want me to know where she is but she's still paying for my phone?"

This was actually the truth, but he didn't know that.

"What about the calls? You send a list of what calls were made every month. Can you print that out for me?"

We each had 2000 free minutes every month. Over sixteen hours. They had to provide a list of calls so we could see that we weren't being overcharged. If I could see the calls my mother was making I might be able to figure out where she was. For instance, if she ordered a pizza there'd be a record of that call, and I could call the pizza place and ask where they were.

"We can send your mother a copy of the bill if she's lost it." When I didn't answer, he said, "I can move your line to an individual account. It will be at a higher price, and we'll need to run a credit check."

"No, thank you."

On Sunday morning, Nana Cole watched the religious programs on TV, since there was no way she was going to church. If you're a normal person, like me, you go out on a Saturday night, and your Sunday morning hangover protects you from TV preachers. Of course, I had no protection other than my iPod and a kitchen that needed cleaning. After lunch, Nana Cole's friends began showing up and I was eventually able to go upstairs... and lessen my anxiety.

When my phone rang at eight-thirty Monday morning I'd already been run ragged. Emerald had been fussy since five-thirty. They say babies can pick up on stress in the air—do they say that? God, I'm not even sure anymore. It certainly seemed like she knew something was up. Friday night we'd been at the ER until after nine and she'd stayed awake the whole time. Then Nana Cole had been snippy all weekend.

Anyway, my cell phone was ringing. I finally answered it. Ham. "Can you get to Three Friends ASAP?" Honestly, it sounded like he was still in that park. Hopefully a park somewhere warmer than Masons Bay.

"Why do I need to go there? I thought the Roberta LaCross thing was finished. You asked for an invoice. Which reminds me how much—"

"Roberta LaCross is dead. You need to get up there before they finish with the scene."

"But... what happened?"

"That's what I need you to find out. Melanie Frasier called me. She's afraid the sheriff thinks she did it. She's hired us to make sure he doesn't arrest her. Oh, crap. I have to go—"

And he hung up. I called Bev and then Jan to come and take care of Emerald, but neither of them was available—to be fair, they'd been there part of Saturday and most of Sunday. That left me no choice. I ran around the house for a good ten minutes collecting everything I was going to need, put the baby in the car seat, grabbed the recently refilled diaper bag, and said good-bye to my grandmother who called out, "Where are you going?"

"Murder!" I called back as I went out the back door. I took the Escalade because I had the baby and I didn't want the hole in my convertible top to blow on her. It was frigid out; it had to be in the low teens, if not lower. I got the baby belted in and then went around to the front, got in, and turned the SUV on. Then I flipped the heater and fan onto high. I revved the engine a few times and then drove down the driveway and turned north.

A damp fog had settled across M-22 so I had to drive slowly. It was a fifteen-minute ride to Three Friends, but it took me half an hour. On the upside, the Escalade was warm and toasty five minutes in.

When I finally got there, the parking lot was full with two sheriff's deputies' black SUVs, a red F-150 and a weird little Subaru—brand-new, yellow, four-door with a pickup bed instead of a trunk. Totally odd.

In front of the tasting room, an area had been cordoned off with yellow crime scene tape—which strangely matched the Subaru. Inside the tape, standing alone and inadequately dressed for the weather, was Detective Rudy Lehmann. He was a tall man with rapidly disappearing sand-colored hair and a frequent look of discomfort in his eyes—which might just have been his reaction to me. The two deputies, both hulking white guys, hung outside the tape looking like KKK members taking a break from listening to the grand wizard.

I pulled in next to the Subaru and turned the SUV off. Now I had a decision to make: I could leave the baby in the nice warm car or I could bring her with me. Both felt wrong. I didn't think I should leave her alone; I also didn't think I should have her out in the cold for long. There are too many situations like this with a baby; two wrong choices and no right one.

Anxiously, I walked around the Escalade, unstrapped the

car seat and pulled it out of the vehicle. I bent over and draped a blanket loosely over Emerald's face. As I walked over to the tape the deputies made a move to stop me, but Lehmann waved them off.

"What are you doing here?"

"I'm working as a private investigator. Melanie Frasier is a client."

"So you show up at a crime scene with a baby?" He was staring at the safety-rated plastic basket hanging from my arm. "That is a baby in there, isn't it?"

"I couldn't find a sitter."

"It's twelve degrees."

"We won't be out here forever. Where's Sheriff Crocker?"

"Florida. He lives there from late fall to early spring."

"He's literally calling it in for half the year?"

"He's up for re-election next year. You want to run against him?"

"Tempting, but no. That's Roberta LaCross, isn't it?" I asked, referring to the body that was rolled up against the glass door. She wore a giant green parka, but even that couldn't disguise that she was a tiny, frail old woman. Faded red-dyed hair popped out of the hood.

"It is."

"Listen, she's suing the winery. Apparently, she fell in the ladies' room nearly two years ago. I've been investigating. The fall was completely her own fault. Really, she has no chance of winning the case. Had."

"I know all that. I've already spoken to Melanie."

"You spoke to my client without me?"

"Yeah, you know she didn't happen to ask for her private investigator. And she didn't ask for a *lawyer*, either."

Okay, maybe that was not a bright thing to say. "Right. Yeah, that makes sense." I thought about what I was looking at then asked, "You don't think Roberta was killed here, do you? It looks like she was dumped."

It was an important point. Obviously, Melanie had a motive. She was being sued. She could have entirely lost the winery. Though if she did kill Roberta, she wouldn't dump her in front of her own tasting room, would she?

"I'm not deciding anything until we know more. There's a forensic guy coming up from Benzie. We've got a sharing arrangement going on with them. And then the medical examiner. He's a consultant, drives in from Traverse." He seemed to remember who I was and added, "Not that it's any of your business."

I looked at the scene and tried to figure out what a forensics guy might find. I mean, there wasn't much. A concrete slab in front of a couple glass doors, with a roof—awning? Portico? Over the whole thing. And, obviously, a corpse.

The concrete had been cleared of snow. There were no ice patches, mainly because of the portico and that they'd used a lot of salt. There were chunks of salt here and there but no ice. There were snowbanks on either side that didn't look capable of telling us anything. There were footsteps everywhere surrounding the concrete, and since we'd only had a dusting overnight they could easily have been customers from the day before.

Then I noticed Melanie waving at me from the other side of the glass doors. She was motioning me around to the side door. I said to Detective Lehmann, "Excuse me. I'd better get the baby inside—"

"One second. Before you go, I should tell you that the Ruperts have come up with a new defense."

The Ruperts were my second or third cousins, Rupert Beckett and his son, Rupert Beckett. They'd murdered my second or third cousin Sammy Hart, and tried to murder me. Yeah, I know. It's a bit of a soap opera. Anyway, they'd already confessed but then recanted and were now considering less truthful options.

"They're saying that Sammy made advances toward them, and they killed him in self-defense."

"He made a pass at them, both of *them*, and so they killed him?"

"That's what they're saying."

"Even if that were true, which I doubt that it is, 'no thank you' works pretty well."

"It gets worse."

"How? How does it get worse?"

"They're saying you made a pass at them too."

"Okay. No. No, no, no. I did not make a pass at both of them or either of them in my grandmother's backyard during a snowstorm with people in the house a few feet away."

That's the part where they tried to kill me.

"*And...* and this is the important part. Neither of them is attractive enough for me to make a pass at in any situation ever. There's no planet anywhere where that would happen."

"Their lawyers found out about your drug use."

I was tempted to erupt like Mount Vesuvius. This place! Could no one keep a secret? Or at least keep a secret about me. Didn't I have any right to privacy? But I did not erupt. Instead, I took a deep breath, and said, "I need to get the baby inside now."

I walked around the building, down a neatly shoveled path and walked in the side entrance. Melanie opened the door for me. Before saying hello, she asked, "Who's this?"

I put the baby carrier up onto the bar. Then slipped the blanket down from her face. I may have woken her because she gave me the dark scowl that always reminded me how much she looked like my grandmother.

"My sister, Emerald," I said, and I touched the back of my fingers to her cheek. She felt warm. In a good way. "Sorry, I couldn't find a babysitter."

I was trying not to say my baby sister since it was pretty

obvious she was a baby. Maybe I'll start calling her my baby sister when she's thirty.

"She looks sweet," Melanie said. The baby looked angry to me, like she hadn't appreciated the blanket over her face. But maybe Melanie was being nice. I dug around and found the plastic keys for Emerald to chew on. I offered them to her, and she snatched them out of my hand. Well, baby-snatch.

"Awwww... aren't you just the best brother. Taking care of your sister."

I smiled modestly. I absolutely agreed with her, but I wasn't going to say so. "Are *you* okay?" I asked with deep sincerity . It seemed an appropriate question.

"I'm fine. I'm not the dead person."

That made me look over to the front door. From this angle I could see the front of the corpse. I couldn't help saying out loud, "Oh crap. I know her."

After Dr. Blinski was murdered in September, I, like many others in the county, tried to get my Oxy from Ronnie Sheck. I'd stood behind Roberta, Bobbie outside his trailer while we waited in line. She talked. A lot. What did she say though? She gave me a tip about a doctor down in Cadillac, a nearly two-hour drive.

"You do?" Melanie asked, looking up from my sister who she'd been shaking the plastic keys at. "You know Bobbie?"

Oh crap. I did not want to tell that story. "Yeah, I've seen her around. Small town." Thinking it a good time to change the subject, I said, "Detective Lehmann said he interviewed you."

"Pretty extensively."

"And that's why you called Ham?"

"I felt like I needed someone on my side."

And we were definitely cheaper than a lawyer.

"They can't possibly think I'd kill someone and leave the body in front of my own business!"

"If it was Sheriff Crocker I'd say yes, absolutely. Detective

Lehmann is a lot smarter, though. Did he ask why you're here so early?"

"He did."

I waited a moment. She didn't elaborate. Instead, she said, "Oh look at those cheeks! I just want to pinch them."

Thankfully, she meant the baby.

"Why are you here so early?" I asked.

"Oh, sorry. I had a client meeting to talk about a wedding. We do summer weddings. Set up tables outside or use the barn if the weather's bad. They didn't show up. I mean, maybe they were early and saw a corpse in front of door and ran for the hills. I don't know. I'll have to call them."

"What time did you get here?"

"Eight."

"And what time did you close last night?"

"Seven."

"So, the body was dumped here sometime between then."

"Well, no. We close at seven, but we don't always leave right away. I think we left closer to eight."

I went over to the door and bent down close to the floor so I could get a better look at Bobbie. The emotion on her face was fear, terror really. It was disturbing, so I tried not to think about it and focused on details. What was I seeing? Her eyes were open and bloodshot. There were tiny red specks all over her face—though they might have been there before. She wasn't wearing makeup. There were a couple of scratches on her neck. Her parka was open, and underneath she wore pajamas.

The bottoms were a solid blue, so I hadn't realized what they were when I'd seen her outside. The top was printed with cartoon sheep jumping around. Counting sheep. Get it? The pajamas had guest starred on *Dawson's Creek* and *Ally McBeal*. I'd tried to get a pair, but they were way out of a barista's budget. How did Roberta pay for—

Maybe that wasn't the important point right now. The

important thing here was that she'd been ready for bed or even in bed when she was killed, meaning it was likely she was killed in her home and brought to the winery to implicate Melanie. I changed my mind about something.

Melanie was back to poking at my sister. Really, it was a bit much. I cleared my throat. "No offense, but it does kind of make sense that you'd dump her body here if you killed her."

"Whose side are on?"

"Yours. But we need to think this through. It looks like she was killed in her home and then dumped here to implicate you. Which is stupid because you wouldn't do that. But that makes it smart. Making it look like someone is trying to implicate you would be smart because it makes you look innocent."

"Is that what Detective Lehmann thinks?"

"Possibly. He asked where you were last night?"

"He did. I was in bed. Alone. My husband and I split a few years ago. He was one of the other three friends."

"Who was the third friend?"

"Eddie Wilton. A close friend of ours. He died in a hiking accident. His parents inherited his portion of the winery. They're like silent investors now."

"So, they stand to lose as much as you if Bobbie was successful?"

"But she wasn't going to win. Not after what you found out."

"True. Did Lehmann ask when the last time you saw Bobbie was?"

"He did, yeah, um... I've seen her around. Main Street Café a couple of times. Bensons. That's about it. How do you think she died?"

"I don't know. I don't see any blood so she probably wasn't stabbed or shot. She might have been suffocated or strangled. But I can't be sure."

"I'm not sure I'm strong enough to strangle another human being. Or schlep a body around."

Honest opinion, she looked strong enough to do both of those things.

CHAPTER EIGHT

Just then, Emerald began to wail. It took a moment to decide if it was her 'let me out of the car seat' wail or her 'I'm hungry' wail. No, it was definitely her 'I'm hungry' wail. It sounded a bit like the alien plant in *Little Shop of Horrors*. An inarticulate 'Feed me, Seymour' or in this case 'Feed me, Henry.' This wail was distinctly different from the more restless 'I need to be changed' wail. Or the far less committed 'I need sleep' wail. And definitely different from the more questioning 'I'd just like some attention' wail.

"Um, the baby's hungry. I've got some formula in the car, let me just grab it."

I didn't leave Melanie any time to object—not that I thought she would have—and just ran outside. I got to the Escalade, opened the back door, grabbed the diaper bag. As I hurried back the deputies stared at me as though they thought I was bringing weapons into the winery.

Back inside, I put the diaper bag on the counter, opened it, and found the bottle of formula. It was cold, very cold. I needed to figure out how to warm it up.

Detective Lehmann came through the door. Apologetically, he said, "I hope you don't mind if I warm up for a minute. We're still waiting on the science team."

"Should I have my lawyer present?" Melanie asked.

I didn't give him a chance to answer, I butted in. "I need to heat this up a little. Do you have a microwave?"

Yes, I know microwaves don't heat evenly and I shouldn't use it to heat formula, but if I shook it really, really well—Melanie must have known all that, because she said, "I can run it under the hot water."

That would have to do. I handed her the bottle and thanked her as she went behind the bar. I asked Detective Lehmann, who was staring at my wailing sister, "I know it looks pretty clean out there, but they'll be able to find fibers on the body or fingerprints on the door, right? Maybe even her skin?"

"It's unlikely they'll find anything at all."

"Then why are we waiting around for a forensics person?"

He shrugged like he didn't know. But then explained, "This is the way crime really works. In a day or two, someone will feel guilty and show up at my office to confess. Or the killer will brag to someone about what they've done, and we'll bring them in and they'll confess. Then they'll get a lawyer, who'll tell them to recant their confession, and we'll have to go to trial. If we go to trial we'll need a forensic report, even one that says nothing was found."

That all sounded a lot like what my cousins were doing. I asked, "How much do you think she weighs?" I asked.

"The baby?"

"Roberta LaCross."

"Oh. Well... she can't weigh much over a hundred."

I glanced at Melanie, who was still holding the bottle under hot running water. It didn't help that Roberta didn't weigh much over a hundred pounds. If a defense attorney tried to say Melanie couldn't have picked her up, the prosecutor would go on and on about the cases of wine she handled on a daily basis.

"How do you think she was killed?" I asked Detective Lehmann.

"I can't discuss that with you."

"Yeah, yeah, yeah… But how *do* you think she was killed?"

"What do you think?"

"I think she was strangled."

"Why do you think that?"

"Because she's got *petruchio* all over her face and a scratch on her neck."

Thank you, *CSI*. Three years of watching every episode just paid off.

"Petechia," he corrected me. "You watch a lot of television, don't you?"

Was he reading my mind?

"A little," I said.

"You know they just make most of that stuff up. Petechia can happen if you cough too much… throw up too hard… A crying jag can give it to you. And then there's about twenty different diseases associated with petechia."

Rude. I tried to redeem myself. "She was killed in her home."

"Why do you say that?"

"I've seen her around. Normally she wears a ton of makeup. And I mean a ton. If she hadn't taken it off, you wouldn't even see the… petechia. Plus, she's wearing pajamas."

Lehmann said, "Excuse me." And walked out of the tasting room.

Melanie came over with Emerald's bottle, and said, "I think this as warm as I can get it."

I lifted my sister out of her car seat, tucked her into my elbow. Her crying had calmed a bit. She might have been enjoying the conversation. Who knows? Anyway, she took the bottle easily and chowed down.

"Isn't she sweet?" Melanie said.

"She's a monster."

"A sweet monster." And then she broke into baby talk riff.

I looked up and could see through the front door that Detective Lehmann had gone over to the deputies and was talking to one of them. After a moment or two, the deputy walked over and got into this black SUV. As it drove off, the detective headed back into the tasting room.

"You sent him off to Roberta's place, didn't you?"

Ignoring me, he said, "Where's her mother? Your mother? Why isn't she taking care of your sister?"

"She flaked. Back in September."

"What does that mean?"

"It means she's gone. We don't know where she is."

"But you know she's okay?"

"She sent some stuff at Christmas. I think she calls my grandmother."

"Is this out of character?"

"It's not. And, no, we don't want to file a missing person's report."

"No problem. Let me know if you change your mind." Then he turned to Melanie, "Look, I should probably warn you. Sheriff Crocker is going to want me to look very, very closely at you. So if there's anything you want to say now..."

"Sure," Melanie said. "There is something I want to say. I'm not talking to you again without a lawyer present."

"That's just going to convince Sheriff Crocker you're guilty."

"Sheriff Crocker is an idiot. Everyone knows that."

Detective Lehmann did not have a good response to that, so he left.

CHAPTER NINE

After Emerald finished her bottle, I put her back in her car seat and she fell off to sleep in a matter of moments. I gave Melanie my cell phone number and told her to call if Detective Lehmann approached her again.

"Do you have a lawyer?"

"Not exactly. We were using the insurance company to fight the lawsuit. If it had gone on, we'd have gotten our own just to make sure the insurance company wasn't screwing us over."

The only lawyers I knew of were Schaub & Schaub, not only because they had represented Roberta, but they had a big sign in front of their offices in Masons Bay. They were available now, but it might still be a conflict of interest.

"Okay, well, let me know when you find someone."

I picked up my sister and left. When I walked into my grandmother's house, I found my grandmother in the living room sitting in her favorite chair. She was watching Court TV.

"Are you supposed to be sitting up?"

"Shhhh. They're talking about Michael Jackson."

The previous month Jackson had been charged with child molestation. An early Christmas gift to Court TV and my grandmother. Something on the TV caught my attention. On screen Micheal Jackson was on top of an SUV dancing around and waving to the crowd.

"What's happening?"

"He was just arraigned."

"He looks happy about it," I said.

"He's happy there are cameras. The whole thing is so disgusting." Which only made it better television.

After a few moments, I said, "I'll make you lunch." I went into the kitchen, carrying Emerald in her car seat. I stopped when I saw a turquoise vinyl and chrome high chair sitting at the table. Nana Cole must have dragged it in from the porch. And here I was worried about her sitting up.

"Is it safe?" I called out to the living room.

"You're here, aren't you?" That was her usual answer when I questioned the things she brought out. Mainly, I asked because if something went wrong and the damn thing collapsed causing Emerald to spend the rest of her life in a vegetative state, I could blame Nana Cole.

On top of that, the baby was getting fussy. I had to get her out of the car seat soon. I unstrapped her and took her over to the high chair. I carefully threaded her into it. Immediately, she began banging her hands against the tray. It might have been a demand for food, but was more likely she'd just discovered she could be annoying on purpose.

I grabbed her toy keys from the car seat and set them in front of her, hoping to distract her. She grabbed hold of them and began banging them against the tray. I'd just made things worse.

There was a ripe banana in a bowl with some other fruit on the table. I grabbed it, pulled a cereal dish out of the cupboard, then mashed up half the banana. In the fridge, I got out a bottle of formula—thank you Dorothy or whoever was here yesterday filling the bottles up—I unscrewed the top and splashed a little in with the banana. Then I mushed all that together. Should it be warm? Did it need to be? I had no idea.

Giving up, I grabbed a baby spoon from the back of the cutlery drawer where it had been waiting since the early eighties, rinsed it off, then sat down next to Emerald. I got some banana mush onto the spoon.

"Nom, nom, nom..." I said, feeling ridiculous. It also didn't work. She stared at me like I was crazy.

"Listen, kiddo, you're going to need to try new things. Today's new thing is banana. Ba-nan-a."

Her mouth dropped open, possibly because I looked like such an idiot, and I popped the spoon in. She grimaced, then moved her jaw around, then looked a little happier, then spit most of the mush out. I scraped it off her chin and popped it back in. Most of it came back out. But then she swallowed.

I scraped off her chin, added a tiny bit more then tried again. Behind me, Nana Cole said, "Should have started that three months ago."

I turned around and stared at her. She was using her cane and gripping the door jam. I asked, "How are you getting around so well?"

"I took a couple muscle relaxers."

"What's a couple?"

"Three. It says on the bottle to take them as needed. I needed three."

"How are you even awake? Don't they make you groggy?"

"I took a little nap while you were gone. Help me sit down."

I put the bowl and spoon on the tray and helped Nana Cole into the seat across from the baby. Behind me I heard the clanging of the spoon hitting the floor. I turned around and saw that Emerald was covered in mashed banana. She'd gotten her hand into the bowl and was now chewing on her banana flavored fist.

"Now look what you've done," Nana Cole said.

"Shut up. She's eating." I walked around and picked up the spoon, rinsed it off in the sink. I debated sitting down and trying to feed Emerald again, but I had the feeling she was swallowing more of it with her hands. I said to my grandmother, "I'll make you a tuna fish sandwich."

"I'd rather have egg salad."

"I'll hard boil some eggs later and you can have one tomorrow."

I set about making the sandwich. She asked, "Where did you go?"

"Do you know Bobbie LaCross?"

"I don't know everyone."

"Well, she's dead. Someone strangled her."

I stirred up the tuna salad and then spread it onto a slice of bread, then put another slice on top. I put the poor example of a sandwich down in front of my grandmother.

"No chips?"

"I'll get some the next time I go shopping." I'd probably been saying that for a month.

She poked at the sandwich and then sighed. I waited for her to say something snide, but instead she said, "She's not actually a LaCross, she just married one. She's a Campbell. They go back in the county further than we do."

A lot of good that did Bobbie. She was still dead.

"Course, they fell on hard times after the war. That's probably why she lets people think she's a LaCross and doesn't correct them."

She took a tentative bite of the sandwich.

"What war?" I asked.

She swallowed hard, then said, "The second world war, what do you think?"

"I think the world is constantly at war so it's good to be specific."

"I need a glass of milk."

As I went to the fridge, I said, "You know a lot about someone you don't know."

"People talk."

As I set a glass of milk down for her, Bev and Barbara came through the back door. Barely stopping to take off their coats, they went right for the baby.

"Oh my gosh," Barbara said. "Look at you covered in your lunch."

"Mashed banana," I said. Mashed banana that was now all over the baby, the high chair and the floor. I decided I should get out of there before someone asked me to clean the mess up. I said, "Excuse me" and went upstairs for a couple Ativan and a long nap.

ABOUT THREE HOURS LATER, I woke up when I fell out of bed. At some point Reilly had shown up and gotten into bed with me. He had a habit of parking himself in the middle of the twin-sized bed and refusing to move, which left little room for me. Which was how I ended up on the floor.

I reached up onto the bed and dragged down a pillow, then I snagged my cell phone off the nightstand. Now that I was cozier, I called Ham and caught him up. When I was finished, he said, "You should go talk to the Wiltons, the other owners. Technically, they're also our client since Melanie is paying us out of the winery's account. Just act like you're updating them."

"They live nearby? She said they were silent partners. I figured they lived somewhere else."

"No, they live up there. Not far from you. I don't know why they're not involved with the winery."

"So they have a motive as well, don't they?"

"Yeah. Or they did until you proved Bobbie was responsible for the fall herself."

"Do you know if they know that?"

"I sent my report to Melanie. Maybe she passed it on. Maybe she didn't."

"So, they might have killed Roberta even though they didn't need to?"

"It's a possibility. Send me an email after you talk to them. We'll figure out what to do next tomorrow."

"Are you in a park?" I had to ask.

"I am."

"In January?"

"I'm watching this dude ice skate."

"Okay."

"He's on workman's comp for a back injury. I've got pictures of him doing a triple axel on two separate days."

It probably wasn't a *triple* axel. That would be Olympic level. But someone on workman's comp probably shouldn't be doing even half an axel. I just said, "Cool."

We hung up and I called information to get the Wilton's address. Then I got up off the floor. Reilly and I made our way downstairs. In the kitchen, Nana Cole was sitting at the table with Bev and Barbara. Emerald was on the floor crawling around.

"Why is the baby on the floor?" I asked. "I don't know how clean that is." I certainly hadn't mopped it. Quickly I snatched Emerald off the floor.

"She needs to crawl around," Barbara said. "She shouldn't spend so much time in the car seat." Then, seeming to realize how critical that sounded, she added, "I know why you're relying on the car seat. It makes perfect sense. I'm just saying... You really *are* doing a wonderful job."

Bev was nodding her head, while my grandmother gave an annoyed snort, then said, "I was telling them about Bobbie LaCross. Barbara used to be in a book club with her."

I bounced Emerald a bit. "Really?"

"Well... she only came a few times, and she didn't read the books. People were annoyed because she talked too much."

"She didn't read the book? What did she find to talk about?"

"She did sort of talk about the books, even though she hadn't read them. One book she was very critical of because she'd dated a police officer, and she knew the author got the policework all wrong."

"She knew that without reading the book?"

"Well, she didn't admit she hadn't read the books. She'd read the jacket and then pretend. Or she'd ask the librarian. Somehow she knew without actually doing the work."

Interesting, but not relevant. I doubted anyone killed her because she was annoying. Tempted, I'm sure, but I didn't think anyone would. I said, "I need to go out, I shouldn't be more than an hour. Will you still be here?"

"Yeah, we're going to make you and Emma dinner."

"I'll probably be back," I said, handing the baby to Bev. "If you want to put her on the floor, at least put down a blanket."

"It's fine," Nana Cole said. "Babies are washable."

THE WILTONS LIVED in Lakeside Heights condominiums. It wasn't an especially inspired name since the complex was built on a hill that looked out at the lake. Halfway between Masons Bay and Bellflower, it sat on the east side of M-22 with a private beach and a handful of docks on the lakeside. The buildings were vaguely colonial, each with two to four units. I drove around the winding streets until I found 114 Bluebird Lane. The Wiltons lived in Unit D.

I got out of my car, tugged down my hat, tossed my piano scarf over my shoulder, and shoved my bare hands into my blue puffer coat. I walked up to their door and rang the bell. After a few seconds, the door was opened by a guy around my age wearing sweats and a sleeveless sweatshirt. He looked me up and down, and said, "Yeah?"

"Is this the Wilton residence?"

"Uh, yeah."

"Oh, are Mr. and Mrs. Wilton available?"

"Who are you?"

"I work for Hamlet Gilbody Investigations. I'm—we're, actually, working for the Wiltons, through the winery. Investigating the woman who was suing them."

"Oh, that bitch. Yeah?"

"Who are you?"

"I'm Tubby Wilton."

Okay, gotta be honest. He didn't look tubby at all. He looked like he'd just come from twelve hours at the gym, thought protein powder and Clif bars were food groups and would have been confused by a Krispy Kreme doughnut, having forgotten that sugar even exists.

"Nice to meet you, Tubby. So, you're..."

"Grandson. I'm taking care of my grandparents. They're not doing well."

"I'm sorry to hear that. I need to give them a report on the case. Can I come in? It's a little cold out here."

Honestly, it wasn't that bad. Not because it wasn't cold, but because there was a lot of heat wafting out of the condo. Tubby stepped back, saying, "You can't stay long. I got things to do."

I stepped inside. At the back of the condo was the kitchen and a powder room, then there were the living and dining rooms in the front, both with amazing views of the lake. There was a stairway that led upstairs to the bedrooms, probably three.

The living room was empty. An oxygen tank sat next to one recliner and a walker next to another. On the floor, along one wall were barbells in different sizes.

"My grandparents are napping. You can give your report to me."

"Um, okay…"

He didn't ask me to sit down. Not that I wanted to. I had the feeling if I did, I might be assigned a random medical device.

"We were able to establish that Bobbie put her foot into the sink to wash off some blood and that was the cause of her fall. Not water on the floor, nor the wine she was drinking."

"So, she's not suing?"

"The suit hasn't been officially dropped. But she also died sometime during the night."

"Bummer." He nodded. Then, "Wow, um, the bitch is dead. Cool."

The bitch is dead really made me want to add a ding-dong, but I resisted. His casual disregard seemed sincere. I mean, if he'd killed her, he'd at least pretend some kind of regret, wouldn't he?

"So… um, do you own part of the winery or is it just your grandparents?"

"It's in a trust. My grandparents and my cousin Cassie. Cassie is Uncle Eddie's kid. She's eight."

That wasn't helpful. The only one physically able to kill Bobbie was Tubby and he didn't have a motive. I mean, it would be a kindness to kill Bobbie for his family, but he wouldn't benefit directly.

Basically, this had been a waste of time. I started to say good-bye so I could get out of there, but Tubby asked, "So, did Melanie kill the bitch?"

"Why do you ask that?"

He shrugged. "I wouldn't put it past her. She's cold-hearted. Uncle Eddie killed himself over her."

"She said your uncle died in a hiking accident."

"He was hiking. But it wasn't an accident. He jumped off a cliff."

"Because of Melanie?"

Honestly, she hadn't struck me as the kind of woman you kill yourself over.

"Yeah, because of her. She was having an affair with Eddie, telling him she was going to leave her husband for him and then she changed her mind. Decided to stay with her husband."

"But they got divorced anyway."

"Well yeah... Uncle Eddie left a long, detailed note."

CHAPTER TEN

I got terribly lost on the way home. In the dead of winter when everything is white, it's not hard to lose your bearings. It was lightly snowing, and I took a right when I should have taken a left—or vice versa, I still don't really know. Normally, it's not that hard getting around. Lake Michigan is to the west. If it was on your left, you were driving north. That meant getting home should have been a snap, since I lived across the street from Lake Michigan.

Of course, there are half a dozen other lakes to contend with. And that might be part of the problem. I think I took a different way out of the condo community that put me on a street behind the complex driving east. Well, mostly east, it was one of those roads that changed direction on a regular basis. When I realized I was lost, I decided to backtrack and try again. That didn't work because I didn't remember where I'd turned onto the road I was on.

Yes, I looked for signs. The street names made no sense. Then I started looking for someone to ask directions, but there really wasn't anyone on the street. It was snowing enough to discourage people from taking a walk but not enough yet for anyone to be out shoveling their driveway. I slowed down a bit and started looking down side streets to see if I could find anyone... or figure out where I was.

After a few miles of nothing, I looked down one road and saw a sheriff's SUV and the funky yellow Subaru. I made a quick turn and slid around a bit. I narrowly avoided going off the road entirely. The Metro did not have winter tires, and I wasn't going to buy them since I'd be leaving soon. It was a very practical decision, one with a harrowing moment here or there.

When I arrived at the property, I pulled in behind the black SUV, managing not to drive into the back of it. Barely. I took a good look at the property. It was a large lot with a good number of buildings on it. In the center was a two-story, white clapboard house with a wraparound porch. It needed a paint job and probably a new roof. On one side, near the road, was a small building that had three doors and three windows. It was some kind of hastily constructed roadside motel from the sixties. Behind the house was a sort of barn, which looked like it might now be inhabited, and beyond that two single-wide mobile homes—one that had had the siding taken off and was waiting to have new siding applied.

Situated behind the mini-motel and next to the main house was an RV trailer, eighteen or twenty feet long. A picket fence peeked out of the snow. Redundantly, crime scene tape was wrapped around the fence. The door to the RV was open, and the one of the deputies I'd seen earlier peeked inside. I got out of the car and tried to figure out how to get to the trailer.

There was a plowed driveway on the other side of the house. Next to the mini-motel and in front of the trailer, a parking place had been plowed. It was empty.

After a moment I saw a narrow path shoveled from the driveway to the gate of the picket fence. Walking up to it, I noticed that the snow was dimpled with footprints, some heavily covered with snow, some barely covered. Some went across the yard to the trailers in back, others to the house. The freshest footprints logically belonged to the deputies, but why had they left the path?

When I got to the gate, the deputy walked over to me. TWISS was written on a nametag that adorned his massive chest. I looked up at him, and asked, "Is Detective Lehmann inside?"

"You don't have any business here."

"Is that a yes or a no?"

"That's a fuck off."

I stood my ground. Fortunately, Lehmann came out of the trailer, so the deputy didn't have an opportunity to crush me like a bug.

Lehmann looked tired. Of course, he hadn't had a three-hour nap in between crime scenes.

"How long have you been here?" I impulsively asked. "It's been hours."

"I was stuck waiting for the foren—you know that's not your business."

"I was curious, that's all."

"Yeah, well, following us around isn't a good idea."

"Actually, I'm lost."

"You're lost? M-22 is a block that way." He pointed in what was apparently an easterly direction.

Okay, that was embarrassing. I'd come awfully close to not being lost all on my own. "Thank you. So, are you finding evidence?"

"Also, not your business."

"You can live in one of these things in the winter?" I asked, meaning the trailer.

"It's got a heater. Now go away."

And I almost did. But as I turned, I realized something important. To Lehmann's back, I said, "She wasn't killed here, you know."

"This morning you said she was."

"I didn't know her car wasn't here."

He turned around and stared at me. "That doesn't mean what you think it means. In the winter, people up here get drunk and drive off the road. Rather than call us and get a DUI, they walk home and go back in the morning to get their vehicles."

"Oh." That was plausible. I'd heard Bobbie spent most nights at Main Street Café. She could easily have driven into a snowbank, walked home, and gotten ready for bed when... bam! Someone's at the door ready to kill her.

"The car can't be far," I said. "She was seventy-something, wasn't she? She couldn't have walked far."

"My deputy's out looking for it."

"Oh. Good idea."

"Is that all, Mr. Milch?"

It was, so I turned and walked down to the Metro. As I walked around to the driver's side, I noticed a middle-aged guy looking out a window in the main house. Dark circles under his eyes, pasty skin. He looked like a creature out of a Stephen King novel, which should have been enough reason to get into my car and drive away. Instead, I walked down to the other driveway and made my way up to the house. I climbed the front steps, which hadn't been shoveled in days, and were icy and thick with snow. I knocked on the front door.

I wondered if he was going to ignore me, but a moment or two later the front door opened a crack. He stared at me. Through those four inches, I could see that he was in his mid-fifties, his hair was thinning and unruly, his eyes a bit yellow. I didn't want to get to close, he looked like he smelled and I didn't want to confirm that.

Brightly, I said, "Hi. I'm Henry Milch."

"Go away."

Not good. I decided to play my one and only card. "I'm Emma Cole's grandson."

"Are you Emily's kid?"

"Well, yeah. When it suits her."

He softened, but didn't open the door any wider. "How is she? We were in the same class in high school."

Okay, not mid-fifties. Forty-three. A very rough forty-three.

"My mom is... great. She just got married."

"Oh," he said, clearly disappointed. I didn't want to break it to him that despite her generally terrible taste in men he wouldn't stand a chance. Then, he rallied and added, "Good for her. Tell her Buford says hello."

"I will. Next time I talk to her. Listen, did the detective ask you if Bobbie had any visitors last night?"

"Nope."

He didn't? That seemed weird. It was such a basic question. Then Buford added, "Didn't talk to me."

"Oh, so he hasn't talked to you yet."

"Didn't answer the door. He shoved the search warrant in a crack. Not much point in talking after that."

"Well, thank you for talking to me."

"Curiosity got the better of me. Didn't know what you was at first."

"I'm a Cole," I said, because it was my only leverage, and because I didn't appreciate being called a 'what'. Seriously, people up here had no idea what to make of a sense of style.

"Yep, always was an odd bunch," he said.

Seriously? This was where he lived, this is what he looked like, and he thought my family was an odd bunch? I decided it was best not to pursue this line of questioning.

"Did you notice if Bobbie had any visitors last night?"

"She's dead? For sure? People keep calling to tell me. I don't want to believe it."

"I saw her body."

He seemed to absorb that like a puff of smoke. Then he said, "My cousin. Second cousin, actually. Once removed. Barely even a relative. Always was trouble. Even as a girl. Destroyed her family, that's what they say. A lot of fighting over what to do about Bobbie. Her mother died round nineteen seventy. After that there was no stopping Bobbie. She got married a few times. Don't even know how many. Three, maybe four. Got arrested a few times but nothing stuck. My dad always thought jail might have straightened her out."

All of that was interesting, but it wasn't what I needed to know. "Did she have any visitors last night?"

"Yep, I think she did."

"Do you know who they were?"

"I didn't know the woman. I don't get out much"

"It was a woman?"

"Well, I think it was. Hard to tell. Had on one of those pillow coats down to her ankles. Could have been a man, I suppose."

"Do you know what time that was?"

"I don't sleep. I try. Every night. But I'm up and down. Up and down."

"What time?"

"Well, after Main Street Café closed, obviously."

"So two, three o'clock in the morning?"

"No. Twelve-thirty."

I could never get used to how early things closed.

"Oh, okay. Is that all you can tell me about the woman you saw? What color was the coat?"

"Coat was purple. Hair was blond."

Uh-oh. Melanie Frasier's hair was blond. And she had a crap alibi. "Did you see what kind of car this person came in?"

"Red pickup."

I remembered a red pickup in the parking lot at Three Friends that morning.

"Was she the only person you saw?"

"Only one I remember."

"Was Bobbie's car here?"

"Don't think so."

"What kind of car does she drive?"

"Some kind of German thing. Old. One of her husbands bought it for her. Long time ago."

"Color?"

"Piss yellow."

Lovely. I chewed my lip for a moment. I knew there was more I should ask, but I couldn't think—

"So did you see if the woman went into the trailer, or did she just drop Bobbie off?"

"Well, she got out of the car, didn't she?"

"I guess she did. Well, thank you for talking—"

"Heard a gunshot, too."

"When? When did you hear a gunshot?"

"Sometime after the woman in the purple coat went into the trailer. It woke me up."

Okay, this was getting messy. At first, he wasn't sure if the woman went into the trailer or not. Now he was saying she did and there was a gunshot. And it woke him up, even though he didn't sleep.

Roberta looked like she'd been strangled. Could she have been shot? I wasn't sure.

"Might have been two gunshots," Buford said, unhelpfully.

CHAPTER ELEVEN

I found M-22 easily enough this time. I drove past our farm and into Masons Bay. When I got to Main Street Café, I began circling the blocks, expanding my search each time I found myself in front of the café. Roberta's twenty-some year-old BMW sat behind what used to be Dr. Blinkski's office.

I parked, got out, and walked around the pale yellow car. I tried to open the doors, but they were locked. Peeking through the frosted windows, I could see that it was a mess inside: take-out bags scrunched up, coffee cups, random totes, a dead plant for some reason.

Checking the outside, I noted a few dents here and there, which was probably not surprising for a woman with alcohol and addiction issues. There was almost an inch of snow collecting on the car. It was still snowing and looked like it might continue for some time.

I got back into the Metro and called Hamlet.

"I have questions," I said when he answered.

"Shoot."

"I just found out that Melanie was at Bobbie's home the night before she was found dead."

"Do the police know that?"

"They will. I'm going to see Melanie and let her know they're going to find out."

"Okay. What's the question?"

"Well... if our client killed someone, do we have to tell the police?"

"Well, first, don't ask her directly if she killed Bobbie."

"Why not?"

"Because we don't want to know that."

"We don't?"

"No. If we know things it can get dicey."

That seemed such an odd thing to say. His job was literally to know things. Still, I said, "Okay. But what if she just tells me?"

"If she confesses to the murder then you need to suggest she talk to a lawyer and turn herself in."

"She won't want to do that."

"Doesn't matter. That's the only ethical advice we can give. We don't help people get away with murder."

"So, if we find out she murdered Bobbie, we stop and go to the police?"

"Uh, yeah, well.... We stop, that's definite. If the police come to us and ask questions we tell the truth. Unless..."

"Unless what?"

"If she hires a lawyer and they hire us, then we have confidentiality."

"What if there's no lawyer and no one asks?"

"We keep our mouths shut. Also, if she confesses, we send an invoice right away." Then he asked, "Do you really think she did it, though?"

Honestly, I hadn't given it much thought. It seemed dumb to kill someone and then drop them at your own door—even if you were trying to fake people out. No matter what, it draws attention to the fact that you have a motive. *And...* Melanie's motive had disappeared. Bobbie would not be taking the winery away from her, so there was no reason to kill her. Unless there was another motive. One I wasn't aware of.

"I don't think so."

"Okay, well, go to the winery and tell her the sheriff's coming soon and that she should call a lawyer."

When I got to the winery, there were more customers than there had been the first time I was there. Word had probably gotten around about the corpse early that morning. I took a spot at the bar. Melanie saw me and nodded. She filled an order and then came down to me.

"Where's your sister?"

"Probably watching Fox News. She's already in love with Sean Hannity."

"Creepy."

"Listen, the police are searching Bobbie's trailer. I talked to Buford Campbell and he told me you were there last night. I'm guessing he told that to Detective Lehmann right after I left."

"Oh shit."

"What were you doing there?"

Keeping her voice low, she said, "I went to Main Street Café to confront Bobbie and ended up driving her home."

"Excuse me?"

"She was drunk."

"Yeah, I've heard that happened a lot. Why did *you* have to drive her home?"

"I went there to tell her off. She'd put me through a lot and I wanted to give her a piece of my mind. But as soon as I started, she crumbled. Telling me how sorry she was. That her life had been so hard. That her last husband had run off with everything she had. That she could barely get by on her Social Security checks. That she was just trying to get money from my insurance company and that'd she'd never have taken the winery. I started feeling sorry for her. She was telling me about all the shitty things men had done to her. I ended up paying her tab and driving her home."

"You got out of the car. When you got to her place you got out of the car."

"Well, of course I did. I was afraid she'd fall and break something, and I couldn't have that now, could I? I'd get blamed all over again."

"You lied to me when you said you were at home."

"Not really. I was at home. Eventually."

She'd also made it sound like she hadn't seen Bobbie in a long time. That was also not true. I let it go. "General question: While you were at Main Street Café did you happen to notice anyone who might have followed you and killed Roberta after you left?"

She looked thoughtful for a moment, then quietly said, "Her son was there."

"Her son? She has a son?"

"They don't get along. In fact, I think they had words. He could be the one who killed her."

"Do you know what the problem was between them?"

"I'm guessing she was a shitty mother."

I felt deeply uncomfortable when she said that. In that particular moment, in a lot of particular moments, I thought I had a pretty shitty mother. I had no desire to kill her, though. I didn't see how it would make the situation any better. Death never made anyone a good mother.

"You told Lehmann you wouldn't talk to him without a lawyer. Were you serious?"

"I feel like I should be."

"You might want to call one," I said, as I watched Detective Lehmann come in the front door.

When she saw the detective, Melanie came out from behind the bar and walked across the tasting room and into what looked like it might be an office.

"Where's she going?"

"To call a lawyer. Did you find Bobbie's car?" I asked.

"We will."

"It's behind Dr. Blinski's office."

He gave me a long, unfriendly look, "Did you touch it?"

"No." I did actually, but we'd talk about that later if we needed to. "I peeked through the windows. She was kind of a slob."

"Her trailer was messy too." Regretting that, he said, "I don't like that you're always around."

"I'm getting paid."

"Not by me."

"What have you found out about her son?" I asked.

"I didn't know she had one."

"Apparently, he was at Main Street Café last night. They fought."

"What's his name?"

Crap. That would have been useful information, but I hadn't asked Melanie. "Um, I don't know."

He smoldered at me for a moment, then said, "If I find out you knew his name and you didn't tell me, you'll be sorry."

"There are at least three people in this room who know. Maybe we should just ask."

Quietly, he turned around and left the winery. I suppose asking a room full of people a question about a murder investigation might not have made him look smart. I certainly wasn't going to do it.

I went home to ask my grandmother.

EMERALD WAS asleep on Bev's shoulder, while Barbara was at the sink doing the dishes. There *was* a dishwasher, but Nana Cole, and now her friends, avoided using it. Something I found confusing since it worked well enough. I used it—

though I caught Nana Cole and her friends rewashing the dishes.

When I walked in, Barbara said, "We have a plate for you in the oven."

I thanked her as I stepped out of my boots, and hung my puffer coat and scarf on a hook near the door. Riley came over and hovered nearby until I spent a bit of time scratching his ears.

"That dog needs a bath," Nana Cole said.

"I'm well aware." I mean, I was inches from him. He really did need a bath. "I'll take him to the groomer in a day or two."

"Just put him in the bathtub and scrub him down."

I tried that. It was not a good idea.

"The groomer clips his nails."

Barbara had gotten my dinner out of the oven and set it on the table. "Sit down and eat your supper."

"Well, just don't put that on *my* credit card," Nana Cole said, meaning the groomer. I intended to do just that. Then to her friends, she added, "Samuel would just spit. Taking a dog to a beauty parlor."

Samuel was my grandfather. She didn't talk about him often. Dinner was an overcooked pork chop, mashed potatoes and peas. Its time in the oven hadn't helped it. I didn't care though, it was still better than what I could cook for myself and I hadn't had to lift a finger.

After my first bite, I asked, "Bobbie LaCross has a son. Do any of you know his name?"

"Of course, we know his name," Nana Cole said but didn't offer it.

"Hal Buckwald," Barbara supplied. "He does odd jobs."

"Whatever happened to his father?" Bev asked.

"He was from the UP," Barbara said. "He wasn't here long. Too citified."

"This? This is too citified?" I said, somewhat appalled.

"You've never been to the UP, have you?"

I shook my head. "And, clearly, I don't want to go."

"It's beautiful up there," Bev said. "You really should see it."

"More trees than people," I guessed.

"Oh, by quite a margin."

"Any idea why Hal was estranged from his mother?"

"They weren't estranged. They just didn't get along," Barbara said.

"Um, actually—"

"We don't really know what goes on between a parent and a child," my grandmother said. "We shouldn't judge."

"Excuse me?" I said, judging was Nana Cole's primary form of exercise.

"Well, Bobbie wasn't a very good mother," Bev said. "I don't think I'm being judgmental when I say that. Her primary interests were men, alcohol and drugs. Usually in combination. That has to be rough on a child."

"It is," I said, bringing conversation to a halt. There they were again, the similarities between Bobbie and my mother were apparent. Well, the men part definitely, alcohol periodically, and drugs, well, there she was an amateur. I was the professional in the family. Oh God... That felt like something I should talk about at a meeting.

Nah. Probably not.

To break the silence, I said to Bev, "Isn't your arm getting tired? If she's asleep you can probably get her into the car seat, and she won't even notice."

"Oh, I'm fine. My nephews are thirty-three and thirty-five. It's been a long time since I've spent this much time with a baby."

Barbara grimaced a tiny bit. It had probably been twenty-some years since she'd held her dead grandson in her arms. She had to be thinking that. I certainly was.

Despite her protests, I took Emerald from Bev and

gingerly tried to get her into the car seat. Of course, she woke up and began fussing almost immediately.

"We can set her up on the sofa," Nana Cole said, referring to the elaborate arranging of pillows we'd devised so she didn't fall off.

"I have to go to Main Street Café."

"You're taking the baby to a bar?"

"Well, I'm not leaving her alone with you."

CHAPTER TWELVE

Like a lot of places in Wyandot County, Main Street Café had once been a private home. As nearly as I could tell, the original building had been a clapboard house, two stories tall with a wraparound porch. At some point, a one-story addition had been made on the side. It had all been painted a sunshine yellow, which was emphasized by the snow piled up around the building.

Inside, the main area had a split personality. The large bar in the center of the room with a TV playing sports made it seem like a bar, but the booths ringing the room made it seem like a restaurant.

Eva Bailey was the barmaid; my mother knew her. But she wasn't there. Instead, there was some guy in his late fifties who seemed to be wavering between a chronic case of alcohol poisoning and cirrhosis.

It was barely seven o'clock and it was fully dark outside. Snow was falling, but no one inside seemed the least concerned. The place was nearly full. I managed to snag two stools at the bar: one for me and one for the car seat. Emerald was already fussing, so I took her out of the contraption and bounced her in my arms. She went from crying to laughing in seconds.

The bartender came down, and as I tried to say I wanted a root beer, he said, "You're Emma Cole's grandson, aren't you? I remember when she used to bring you in here. You were about the same age as this one. What's her name? I know someone told me but I—"

"Emerald."

"Ah. Pretty name. What's her last name?"

Honestly, I had no clue. And that had been a problem since my mother had run off with the baby's birth certificate. She used the name Fetterman, her second husband's name, so Emerald Fetterman was a possibility. I was Milch after her first husband, though he wasn't my father. So Emerald Milch was unlikely. The baby could have her father's last name, even though they married after she was born. That was Hounsell. Emerald Hounsell. That was a terrible name, so I made an executive decision, the same one I'd been making for months, and said, "Cole. Emerald Cole."

"Lovely name. Did you want something?"

"Yes, I'll have a root beer."

While he walked a few steps down the bar to get it, I looked around. Something was going on. At the far end of the bar a middle-aged guy stood on a bar stool messing with the back of the TV. The kind of guy you took one look at and knew he'd been divorced at least twice, had children with several women, and was swamped by child support payments. Near his feet sat a laptop with a microphone next to it. God, I hoped it wasn't karaoke.

The bartender was back with my root beer and a maraschino cherry for Emerald. Cherries aren't mushy enough for a baby, so I said, "Oh, she's a little young..." But it was too late, she'd already taken the cherry out of his hand and was putting it into her mouth. I didn't know she could actually do that. Since I knew how maraschino cherries were made I wanted to snatch it away from her, but she already had most of it in her mouth. Of course, she wouldn't be able to chew it. *Could you gum a cherry?* I had no idea.

I was waiting for her to spit it out, when someone tapped me on the shoulder. I turned around and there was the girl from the fudge shop, Zoey Calder. She didn't look as awkward. Maybe it was the fact that she wasn't wearing a red-and-white smock.

"Hi! Are you here to play trivia? Do you wanna join our team? Please, please, please... Join our team."

"Um, I don't know..." I turned back to the baby and looked for the cherry. Emerald wasn't chewing. Had she swallowed it? She couldn't have. She'd have choked. Oh God, did she need the Heimlich? There was a chart on the doctor's wall. I'd almost read it—

"Your baby is adorable."

"What? No, no, no... god no. She's my *sister*."

I wanted to yank open her jaw and stick my fingers in her mouth, but it seemed like a bad time.

"That explains the family resemblance."

Family resemblance? She's a blob with a tuft of hair. I mean, I hoped Emerald would take after me at some point, but at that particular moment—

"So what about it? It's going to start in a minute or two." Then Zoey leaned in close and said quietly, "Patty brought this guy, I think she's trying to set us up and it's a hard no on my end. You'd be helping me out."

I glanced over at the table. There were Patty Gauthier and a guy in his early thirties. Honestly, he wasn't that bad. Dark with a heavy beard and a few extra pounds. With the right lighting, though... Besides, Zoey worked in a fudge shop. She couldn't really have prospects. Could she?

"Uh, yeah, sure..." I said, mostly because it might be a good idea to talk to Patty again. I stood up, picking up the baby as I did and the cherry fell out of her lap—where I hadn't noticed it, and landed at my feet.

Thank god. Cancel the baby Heimlich.

Tucking Emerald into the crook of my elbow, I picked up the root beer with one hand and the diaper bag and car seat with the other. Taking care of a baby meant holding onto more things than you ever thought possible. As I got settled at the table, I said, "This is my sister, Emerald," before they could ask.

I decided this must be an important social event for Patty. She'd taken her hair out of its braid, and it was now in a bun sitting artfully atop her head with strands falling out here and there. She wore a creamy Irish sweater and a lot of blush.

Patty said, "Hello again. This is my next-door neighbor, Brian Belcher."

I smiled sympathetically at Brian. His life must have been hell from grade school to high school graduation. Probably much worse than mine. Belcher, Milch. We might have been friends.

He glanced oddly at Patty, then asked me, "Are you good at this?"

"Yeah, I guess." I mean, I went to college, right?

"Good. Usually we suck."

"That's mainly because Bobbie always insisted on the wrong answer," Patty said. "Not to speak ill of the dead."

"She did though," Brian agreed with her.

The guy with the laptop at the bar introduced himself as Ed, and said, "We're going to have a good time tonight, as long as none of my ex-wives show up."

Nailed that one.

He blathered on about the rules, which I didn't really pay any attention to. Then he rattled off the teams. We were the Boomers. There were also the Boozers, the Boogiemen, the Bookworms... I was sensing there was a theme the night this all began.

Emerald looked sleepy. Well, she was usually asleep at this time of night. I tried laying her on my shoulder the way Bev had. I probably wouldn't be able to keep it up as long as she had, but I might as well give it a try.

"Okay, let's start round one with science!"

My team groaned.

Ed read the question off the screen. "On the periodic table Pb is the symbol for: 1. Polonium, 2. Phosphorus, 3. Promethium or 4. Lead."

My team leaned in, keeping and their voices low so the other teams wouldn't hear us.

"Well, it's not lead," Zoey said.

Patty nodded her head in agreement, saying, "I don't think promethium is actually a thing."

Brian shrugged and said, "I have no idea."

Then they all looked at me.

"It's lead."

Even though I'd had chemistry in high school, I didn't remember what was and wasn't on the periodic table. I did however remember how to take a multiple-choice test.

"Because it begins with L, they think you're going to immediately reject it. It's a trick. And..." I kind of remembered this and I kind of didn't: "The original elements didn't always have letters that corresponded to their names. Elements added later do. So, promethium is something like Pm."

They looked at me suspiciously, then Zoey wrote down my answer, Lead, and took it over to Ed.

I looked around the room as we waited. The librarian, who I called Hanging Chad was there in a booth with three other players. I pegged them as the Bookworms. The only other person I recognized was the spooky girl who saw auras and said strange things. I couldn't remember her name. She was with the Boogiemen.

Ed announced that there were ten seconds left to get the

answers in, and the Boogiemen ran their answer up. Then Ed began teasing us with the answers.

"Okay, so it's not promethium or polonium. And it is... lead."

My team gave me a thumbs up. Well, Patty and Zoey did. Brian was kind of stoic. The Bookworms were cheering themselves, so they must have gotten it right as well. When Ed began to read the results, we were tied with them at ten points. The other teams had gotten it wrong.

The next question was, How many Grammys has Madonna won? I didn't even have to wait for multiple-choice. Not that I was a superfan. I prefer Kylie, but I had been in enough conversations about Madonna to know the answer was five even before the choices were read out.

I took the opportunity to lean into Patty and ask, "You told me Bobbie killed a man. Can you tell me more about that?"

She blushed, full-on fire engine red. "Oh gosh. I was just being dramatic. I should never have said that."

"But you did say it. What did you mean?"

"Nothing. I was being unkind."

"Where were you Thursday night?"

"I beg your pardon?! That's none of your business."

Zoey nudged me, and asked, "What do you think? I think seven."

The choices were: 0, 1, 5 and 7.

"Five," I said.

"Really? You're sure?"

"Yes."

Zoey wrote down the answer and ran it up to Ed.

Patty leaned in and said, "I have an alibi, since you asked. I just don't see why I should have to tell you. You're not a policeman or anything."

"I don't believe you."

"It doesn't matter if you believe me. I have an alibi."

"Yeah, you probably do. I don't believe you were being

dramatic when you said Bobbie killed a man. I think you meant it. And I think you should tell me who she killed. And how she got away with it."

Now she paled and looked frightened. She glanced at Brian as though he might rescue her, but he was cringing as Zoey hooted loudly because the answer was five, just like I'd said.

Patty got up and walked away. Odd, very odd.

Ed announced that we were still tied with the Bookworms and that none of the other teams had any points. I leaned over and said to Brian, "So, you're Patty's neighbor?"

He looked surprised that I'd spoken to him, and said, "And friend. She's always been kind to my family."

That could mean a lot of things. I bit my tongue, and said, "Yeah, people up here are really nice."

"Oh they are, aren't they?" Zoey agreed.

"Not everyone," Brian said.

"Really?" I said, hoping he'd elaborate. He didn't. "Did you know Bobbie LaCross?"

Zoey giggled. "Everyone knew Bobbie."

"She lived next door with Patty for a long time," Brian said. "Too long."

"The next question is, Which constitutional amendment protects against self-incrimination? The First, the Second, the Fourteenth or the Fifth."

I rolled my eyes. Could this really be that easy? Before I could provide the answer, Brian said, "Fifth."

Zoey nodded enthusiastically, wrote down the answer. I asked Brian, "Was Bobbie one of the people who aren't really nice?"

"You're awfully nosey."

"He's a private investigator," Zoey explained for me. "He's working for the winery Bobbie was suing."

"Isn't that over? Since she's dead."

I nodded, then added, "Also, because she was lying."

Just then Emerald shifted in her sleep and wrapped a tiny arm around my neck in a little hug. I tried to ignore how much I enjoyed that. I was also trying to ignore how much my arm had begun to hurt and the fact that it time to change her diaper.

"Where's the men's room?"

Brian pointed. I picked up the diaper bag and left. Well, they had it in hand, so I didn't see the point of waiting for a break. Was there a break? I had no idea. If it was karaoke you'd just leave when someone bad was singing, which was basically any time you wanted. But this... Not like I had much choice. One of us was really beginning to stink.

Before I got to the men's room, I ran into aura-girl. She was thin, brunette, and had a had a habit of wearing obviously homemade clothing. Tonight's piece was a thick woolen sweater with one arm longer than the other. Sandy? Yeah, that was it, Sandy something. She took one look at me and Emerald, and said, "Oh my... I'm so happy for you!"

"She's not mine. She's my sister."

"No, I meant your aura. It's blue. You're content and at peace."

Actually, at that particular moment I was a little frantic. Changing diapers was not on my list of things that brought me joy and contentment. She continued, "You must have taken what I said very seriously."

"Yeah, what did you say again?"

"I said you're a student of life. You remember that, I'm sure you do."

"To be honest, I really didn't understand what you meant. It sounds cool but, you know, it's kind of vague."

"A student of life? What could be clearer? You're interested in people, you like watching them, figuring them out. Solving them in a way. And it's good for you. Very good."

Some of that wasn't far off; she was giving me the creeps. "I hate to interrupt, but my sister needs to be changed."

"Of course, of course..."

But then I thought, since I had the chance, "Did you happen to know Bobbie LaCross?"

She darkened. In fact, I felt like I was watching her aura change colors before my eyes. "I hate to say bad things about people. It's not good... karmically."

"Thinking them can't be much better," I said, hoping to nudge her into saying whatever it was. But she turned and walked away. Well, people seemed to have strong opinions about Bobbie.

In the men's room, there was just enough room on the sink to balance Emerald while I removed one disposable diaper and got her into another one. One thing my grandmother taught me, which was actually helpful, was that you had to keep one hand on the baby at all times. It kept them from rolling, slipping, sliding, tumbling, flipping, spinning or otherwise escaping your grasp.

I was applying some ointment, when Hanging Chad came into the restroom. He didn't bother with any of the traditional uses of a public toilet, and said, "The books you reserved are in. They've been in for quite a while. I tried calling you, but you don't answer."

As I quickly finished diapering my sister, I tried to figure out what he was talking about. I had a vague memory of going to the library shortly after my mother *abandoned* us and trying to take out a couple of books on baby craft. *What to Expect When You're Expecting* was one of them—a complete misfire, as I later found out it was only about pregnancy and not useful at all. Honestly, I don't remember what the other books were. Between detoxing and actually taking care of Emerald I'd completely forgotten about the books. Between the baby brigade, the pediatrician and some very enlightening baby blogs, I'd pretty much gotten a handle on things. At least I hoped so.

"Ah, yeah, um thanks. I'm not sure I need them anymore."

Given the extra lousy job I'd done diapering Emerald, I thought for a moment he might disagree.

"Then I'll release them back into circulation."

He started to leave the restroom which left me wondering, had he really followed me into the men's room to tell me my books were in? But then he stopped and asked me, "Hey maybe you'd like to have coffee some time?"

Oh, god.

"I kind of have my hands full at the moment." Literally, I was holding an infant.

"Oh, well, yeah. Okay. Sure. Maybe sometime... in the future."

"Probably not."

"Oh. Yeah, right."

And then he left.

You might think I was rude, but really I wasn't. The last thing I wanted to do was lead him on. Saying no isn't always as impolite as it sounds. I know I might have, possibly, flirted with him a little tiny bit to get information. I mean, seriously, who hasn't flirted with a librarian when confronted with the Dewey decimal system? Anyway, I was sure he'd get over it.

When I got back to the table, my teammates were looking glum. In my absence they'd missed two questions. Ed read the next question. "In the *Brady Bunch*, who was Cousin Oliver? 1. Alice's love child, 2. Greg Brady's best friend, 3. Carol's nephew or 4. a kitten the family adopted."

"Well, obviously not number one," I said.

"It's the kitten, isn't it?" Zoey guessed.

"No. It's not. It's Carol's nephew."

I mean, didn't they watch television at all? *The Brady Bruch* was propping up at least two cable networks. And Patty was old enough to have seen it when it came out.

To my surprise, she leaned over and said, "Oh look, there's Bobbie's son, Hal."

I followed her stare across the room. I'd expected someone

around my age, but this guy was around fifty, had lost most of his hair, had deep set haunted eyes and had obviously seen some hard times. A lot of hard times.

I was reminded again of the similarities between our mothers—yes, I know that's coming up a lot. Then Hal smiled at someone, revealing that he had less than ten teeth. Despite my mother's obvious and persistent flaws, she had always provided dental care. Or at least her various boyfriends had. In fact, she'd nearly married a dentist so I could have braces.

I was about to get up and go talk to him, the words, "Could you watch—" had come out of my mouth, when Patty cryptically said, "Detroit."

"Detroit? What about Detroit."

"That's where Bobbie killed a man. In a bar."

I watched her carefully. This didn't feel like the truth. This felt like something she was making up.

"So, what? She got in a knife fight?"

She shook her head. "This guy tried to drug her, put something in her drink. She figured it out, so when he looked away she switched the drinks. He drank it and died."

She'd just made the knife fight sound more believable. "So he was trying to drug her... to have sex with her?"

"I guess."

"And that amount of whatever the drug was killed him?"

She shrugged. "All I know is what Bobbie told me."

I still didn't believe her. She never would have told me that Bobbie killed a man if this was the story. And even if she did, why would she try to take it back? Well, maybe because she was embarrassed that she'd told me something so obviously untrue. But then, tonight, she was trying not to tell me. This didn't feel like the kind of story she'd try to hide.

And then Detective Lehmann walked in.

CHAPTER THIRTEEN

We won. Emerald had begun screaming because she was hungry. I got the bartender to run her bottle under hot water and popped it into her mouth. She spent the entire second round finishing the bottle. Meanwhile, we crushed it. We'd caught up and were now sixty points ahead of all the other teams.

Detective Lehmann, who'd come with his pretty wife, Gloria, got the last empty booth in the place. He had a draft beer while she had an appletini. They didn't seem to talk much, mostly he was watching us all. Or maybe not all of us. Maybe just me.

The game finished up. We won, which meant we got a gift certificate, twenty bucks, to come back to Main Street Café for dinner. I had no intention of socializing with these people, so I hurried out of there as quickly as possible. On the ride home, I was grateful for my grandmother's SUV. The snow was thick and wet and coming down fast. I clutched the steering wheel tightly, while my sister sat in her car seat, happy for once, discovering that she had fingers.

The next morning—and I do mean morning, it wasn't even seven yet—I was still in my UCLA blue-and-yellow pajamas and had just finished feeding Emerald. Her first experience of apple sauce. She seemed to like it. Anyway, what I'm trying to get to is that there was a sudden pounding on the front door. When I got there, I opened the door and there stood Detective Lehmann.

Without a hello or 'how ya doing' he said, "I need you to come with me."

I didn't like the sound of that, so I said, "I'd rather not."

"Fine. Henry Milch you're under arrest for interfering with a sheriff's investigation. If you come with me peaceably I won't cuff you."

Then he read me my rights, which were extremely boring, especially for something that important. When he was done, I said, "I can't leave my sister alone with my grandmother. She's not well enough to take care of a baby. Can you come back at noon? There will be someone here then."

"No, I can't come back at noon! You're being arrested."

"Yes, I understand that. But it's not convenient."

"It's not meant to be."

"I'm fairly certain Michael Jackson was allowed to make an appointment when he turned himself in. And I'm fairly certain you're not here about child—"

"You're not Michael Jackson."

"Well, no, I'm not. I like older men."

"I'm on the verge of cuffing you."

"Okay. Come inside. I can change out of my pajamas, can't I?"

He signed heavily and stepped into the house. I started toward the stairs but stopped when he asked, "Do you have guns in the house?"

"I don't think so. You've got two of my grandmother's weapons. You'll have to ask her if she's got any more. She's in the kitchen." Then, before I went up the stairs, I asked, "Is there going to be a mug shot? Because if there is, I'd like to wash my hair, maybe shave."

"You have five minutes."

I rolled my eyes at him and went up the stairs, wondering what I should wear to be arrested. As I stood in front of my closet, I imagined Martha Stewart giving me advice: 'Comfort is the order of the day whenever one is arrested. Loose-fitting jeans or even sweats are appropriate. A bulky sweater over a simple tee is wise, as holding facilities can vary widely in temperature. No jewelry, of course. The guards will only take it away from you and are likely to share amongst themselves. And definitely nothing constraining around the wrists. Handcuffs are constricting enough.'

I should probably take this more seriously, I thought, as I pulled on a pair of purple sweats. But it was hard to take being arrested seriously when, on the one hand I hadn't done anything, and on the other if I hadn't refused to be questioned he wouldn't have arrested me at all.

I finished dressing: a black-and-pink plaid flannel shirt and my trusty lime-green sweater. When I got downstairs to the kitchen, Detective Lehmann was chatting pleasantly with my grandmother.

"How long have you been up here?" she asked him.

"Three years."

"Your people in Grand Rapids must miss you."

"I get down to see them often enough."

I picked an apple-sauce-covered Emerald out of the high chair and plunked the car seat onto the table so I could put her in there.

"Oh, you don't need to do that," Nana Cale said. The baby was already getting cranky.

"Yes, I do. Call around and get one of the girls to come over. I'm being arrested and I have no idea how long I'll be."

"Arrested? You said you'd stopped doing drugs."

"I'm being arrested for interfering with their investigation."

To Lehmann she said, "He never could mind his own business."

That wasn't exactly true. I was minding my own business quite well in Los Angeles. It was only when I got—hey wait a minute. No one in Northern Lower Michigan minded their own business. She really was being unfair.

"Call Hamlet for me."

"What's his number?"

"Call information in Grand Rapids. Hamlet Gilbody Investigations."

"They charge for information."

"Nana, I'm being arrested. Spend the quarter."

"You're two seconds away from being cuffed."

I grabbed my puffer jacket, my piano scarf and my floppy eared hat, and said, "I'm ready, okay?"

We went out the backdoor and walked through the paths I'd shoveled, sloppy but functional, over to a black Ford Explorer with SHERIFF in big gold letters on the side. Detective Lehmann opened the back door and I climbed in. A glowering deputy sat in the driver's seat. When Lehmann got into the passenger's seat and shut the door, I said, "They don't let you drive?"

Neither of them said a word. This was going to be cheery.

We were at the end of the driveway and about to turn onto M-22, when the deputy asked, "Why isn't he cuffed?"

"It's not necessary," Detective Lehmann said.

"Sheriff said—"

Ah, that was what was going on. Crocker had reached out a long arm from Florida and messed with Lehmann's investigation. No wonder he was grumpy.

The sheriff's office was part of the Wyandot County Municipal Center. A group of three contemporary brick buildings which in addition to the sheriff's office and jail, housed court rooms, clerks, commissioners and various others who did the mysterious work of a county.

I had the distinct feeling my cousins were still in the jail section of the sheriff's department. They hadn't been able to make bail—the point of making it so high, one million each—so they had to be somewhere. Fortunately, I was not put in a cell with them. I was instead led to the maple-paneled interview room, which I'd been in before. Fun times.

Detective Lehmann got us both coffees. I had mine with plenty of sugar and artificial creamer—the kind that came from artificial cows. He sat down, and without any kind of ice breaker asked, "Has Melanie Frasier admitted to killing Bobbie LaCross?"

I was still a little fuzzy on what I could and couldn't say. But the honest answer was actually beneficial to my client, so I said, "No. Can you ask me questions about my client?"

"I can ask you anything I want."

"But do I have to answer?"

"Are you working for her attorney?"

"Nnn—yes."

"Are you? Or aren't you?"

"I'm not sure."

Well, it *was* confusing. First, we were working for Melanie's insurance company. Then we were working directly for Melanie. She hired a lawyer so maybe we were working for them now. For all I knew there was an email at home explaining all that.

It was possible.

"Can you tell me why Melanie killed Bobbie?"

"She didn't kill her. How can I tell you the reason for something that didn't happen?"

"But Melanie did have a motive?"

"No, I told you, we caught Bobbie in a lie. There was no way the lawsuit was going to proceed. It was all over. Melanie didn't have a reason to kill her."

"So what was she doing at Bobbie's place the night she was killed?"

"She said she went to the bar to tell Bobbie off, but then she ended up feeling sorry for her. Bobbie was drunk and went full-on pity party, so she drove her home and made sure she got into the trailer safely."

"None of that sounds likely."

"Which part? The part where Melanie was being kind? Or the part where Bobbie was being manipulative."

That earned me an icy stare.

"Tell me everything Brian Belcher said to you."

"Brian Belcher? Why are you interested in Brian Belcher?"

"He was sitting right next to you. He must have said something."

"Mostly that Patty was really nice to his family." Then something hit me. I did have information he'd find interesting. Possibly useless but information none-the-less. "Patty told me Bobbie killed a man."

"Go on."

"She said it the first time I talked to her, which would have been before Bobbie was killed. Then last night she said she was just being mean. Then she told me a story about Bobbie killing a man in Detroit who was trying to drug her by swapping drinks. I didn't believe it."

"What do you believe?"

Good question. I thought about it a moment. "I think the first thing she said was probably true. But now she wants to cover it up because it might have something to do with Bobbie's being killed."

"Do you think Patty killed her?"

That hadn't occurred to me. She seemed to have gotten Bobbie out of her life. Did she still have a motive?

"If Bobbie had still been living with her, I'd say yes. But Patty got rid of her last spring."

He frowned at me. After thinking for a moment, he said, "She was probably being mean when she said that. By the end of their friendship, they hated each other. That's right, isn't it?"

I nodded.

"It's sounding like a common theme in Bobbie's life."

"Did you talk to Hal Buckwald last night?" he asked.

"No. Should I have?"

Actually, I'd wanted to. I hadn't because Lehmann was sitting in the back booth, and I didn't want him seeing me talking to the victim's son. I would have said that, but he'd have used it as evidence that I knew what I was doing was wrong. It wasn't wrong, but I knew he'd think so. Which almost made it wrong.

"You've been asking questions about him though."

Should I have been? Was he Lehmann's main suspect?

"Was he seen near Bobbie's place the night she died?"

"Where did you hear that?"

"I didn't. I'm asking if *you* heard it?"

"I didn't hear it. The only person seen at Bobbie's was Melanie Frasier."

"A lot of people live on the Campbell property."

"No one saw anything."

"Yeah, but maybe one of them killed Roberta."

There was a knock on the door and the deputy who'd driven us over said, "Rudy, there's a lawyer out here. Bernie Schaub."

"Junior or Senior?"

"Junior?"

"What's he doing here?"

"Says this one works for him."

This one was me.

"Excuse me, I'd like to see my investigator," Schaub said, pushing his way into the room. Of course, I'd never seen him before in my life. He was barely older than I was and looked a lot like Dennis the Menace after a mild puberty. He wore a gray three-piece suit that he hoped to grow into.

He asked Detective Lehmann, "Are you charging Mr. Milch?"

"I'm considering it."

"What are the possibilities?"

"Interfering with a criminal investigation."

"Melanie Frasier is my client, and since you seem to think she's a murderer, Mr. Milch has been investigating. That's not interfering. That's mounting a defense."

"She hasn't been charged yet."

"And hopefully you'll have enough sense not to charge her at all. Have you been asking Mr. Milch questions about Ms. Frasier?"

"Of course."

"You'll need to stop that. Attorney client privilege extends to investigators."

I could see that Lehmann was clenching his jaw over and over. Finally, he turned to me and said, "Get the fuck out of here."

Once we were in the parking lot, Bernie led me to a Volkswagen Jetta. It was a couple of years old, dark blue with a camel interior. There was six inches of snow still on the roof, which meant he didn't have a garage to put the car into. There was a dent in the front fender, and when I opened the door the interior was filled with junk mail, bags from fast-food places (indicating he did some traveling, as there were no franchises in Wyandot County) and empty plastic water bottles. I thought he might apologize for the state of the car, but as soon as the doors were shut, he asked, "What did he ask about Melanie?"

"Uh, well, he asked if she might have a motive other than the lawsuit."

"And you said..."

"I said, I didn't think so."

"What else?"

"Mostly I said she didn't kill Bobbie LaCross. Because I don't think she did."

I noted that Bernie didn't rush to agree with me. "Did he ask about anyone else? Anyone he might consider a suspect?"

"He saw me at trivia. He asked about the people I was sitting with. Patty Gauthier and Brian Belcher."

"Patty's my aunt. My mother's sister."

"So, she probably isn't the killer."

"I didn't say that," he said with a shrug. "She could be, who knows. Who else did he ask about?"

"Bobbie's son, Hal Buckwald."

"Interesting."

"Can I ask a question? You represented Bobbie LaCross. Isn't this a conflict of interest?"

"My father represented Bobbie. He and I don't communicate."

"Ah... a Chinese wall," I said, knowingly. I'd picked up the term from *L.A. Law* or *The Practice* or *Ally McBeal*. I couldn't remember which. It referred to a situation where members of the same firm represented opposing parties.

Bernie looked confused, and said, "I don't know what that is."

"It's where you don't communicate with your father about cases that might have a conflict—"

"You misunderstood. I don't communicate with my father. Full stop."

"But it's Schaub & Schaub?"

"I'm aware of that. Very aware."

"That must be hard on your secretary." I doubted the firm could afford a secretary for each of them. We were in the wrong kind of German car.

"Not really. If my father and I need to communicate we email. It's not always civil, but it gets the job done."

"May I ask what the problem is?"

"No, you may not." Without a pause he said, "I'm going to need a list of everyone you've spoken to since you took the original case and notes on what was said."

Crap. This was a job with homework. "Can't we just find the killer?"

"It probably isn't necessary. They haven't arrested Melanie, which means they don't have enough evidence. If they don't find anything else, the whole thing might blow over."

"Really? You have met our sheriff, haven't you?"

"True. But it's not an election year. I suspect he'd like this to go away. Heaven forbid he should have to come back from Florida."

"What happens if she's arrested?"

"Then we'll look at other suspects. Ones the sheriff ignored. If it goes to trial, we'll want to show that someone other than Melanie could have done it."

"Expose the real killer."

"It doesn't have to be the *real* killer. It just has to be a plausible *other* killer. We just have to create reasonable doubt."

"Finding the real killer would do that, wouldn't it?"

Okay, okay... I was getting a little addicted to finding killers. It was exhilarating and exciting, and yes, it was also dangerous, and I could potentially end up dead. Actually, it was a bit like... well, OxyContin.

Setting that uncomfortable realization aside, I pointed to our driveway and told Bernie to turn into it. Fortunately, our plow guy had come and we were able to get almost all the way to the house. It was still snowing enough that he might have to come back.

Before I got out of the car, he said, "Don't forget I need that list."

"I won't forget."

"Tomorrow afternoon."

"What about tomorrow afternoon?"

"Do you think I could have the list by then?"

"Oh, okay, well, sure..." Then I added, "I'll do my best." Which most people would rightly interpret as a no.

"Great, I look forward to it."

I climbed out of the car, noting that Bev's Cherokee was

right there. Someone, probably Bev, had shoveled a path from the driveway to the back door. That was normally my job, so I was happy someone else had done it.

Kicking my snow-covered boots on the doorjamb, I stepped into the kitchen. Bev and Barbara were at the table with my grandmother. Emerald wore a half a cup of rice cereal, which didn't seem to be bothering anyone. Riley was asleep in his dog bed. The room was strangely quiet. I could hear the Colonial-style wall clock ticking. It was barely eleven.

Once I was down to my socks, I went to the sink and wet a clean washcloth. Then I went over to the baby and began cleaning her up. I glanced up at Nana Cole to see that her face was rigid. Bev and Barbara's faces were just as rigid. Something had happened. But before I could ask what, Bev stood and said, "We'll be leaving then."

"Um... you couldn't stay until Jan gets here? That would really..."

"I'm sorry, not today," Bev said. No one was looking at me. They walked over to the back door; then put on their boots and coats in silence. I looked at my grandmother and pulled a questioning face, which she ignored. As soon as they were out the door, I asked, "What was that about?"

"I called Bev right after you left, right after seven this morning." Her tone was filled with disgust. "They came right over."

"Why is that a problem?"

"*They*. They were together."

"Right. So they were having—" I was about to say breakfast when I realized. They were *together*. Okay, I should have picked up on that. It was a major gaydar malfunction. Not that my gaydar was particularly attuned to lesbians, but still, I should have—of course, they *were* friends of my Nana Cole, which meant queerness was not even a possibility. And they were old. What were they doing having *sex*? With anybody? Oh god, don't even think about it. I stopped cleaning the baby.

Really, she didn't seem to mind being sticky and this was kind of important.

As reasonably as possible, I said, "You know that has nothing to do with you, don't you?"

"Of course it has to do with me. They told me. Why did they have to tell me?"

"You said you figured it out."

"They could have lied. That's what friends do for each other."

"Nana, you matter to them. God knows why." Her eyes flashed at me. I decided to plunge forward. "If you don't know then you don't really know them. Is that what you want?"

"People should be what they're supposed to be."

"Who decides what they're supposed to be?"

"God."

"And you know what God wants?"

"I go to church. I read my Bible."

"And what if the minister's wrong? What if you misunderstand the Bible? It's certainly contradictory."

B minus, Comparative Religion 34. Proud of that. I even went to most of the classes.

"I know what's true in my heart," Nana Cole said.

"Yeah, well, what if what's in your heart is meanness and hatred? Is that what God wants?"

"They're going to hell. You're going to hell. Is that really what *you* want? Would you really give up eternity for... *acceptance?*" She said acceptance like it was a dirty word.

"I've seen what Christians are like. If heaven's full of them, then I don't want to go."

I mean, seriously, an eternity with people shaming each other over impure thoughts versus disco inferno 24/7? It seemed an easy decision to me.

With a grimace, Nana Cole stood up from the table. Her cane was right there at the ready. I watched as she hobbled down the hallway to the living room, cane in one hand, the other bracing her against the wall. She looked frail, easily broken. I realized we'd grown up in very different worlds.

She'd been welcomed into the world and given the prescribed roles of wife and mother; both seemed to have fit her well. I grew up in a world that did not welcome me. In fact, all too often it encouraged me not to exist at all. Somehow, my struggling to find a place, and now Bev and Barbara doing the same, somehow that threatened Nana Cole. It didn't change her position in the world, but somehow she felt it did.

God, I needed a thirty milligram OxyContin. Two would be better. Unfortunately, I was going to have to settle for an Ativan. I finished cleaning up the baby, wiped down the high chair, and then took Emerald upstairs. I changed her diaper—it was overdue—and put her into the crib, hoping she'd take a long nap.

My grandmother hadn't asked me anything about being arrested or how I got un-arrested. I guess that just showed how upset she was. Selfishly, I wondered what we were going to do without Bev and Barbara. Together, and separately, but mostly together, they'd been doing a lot of child-care. I watched my sister as she lay in the crib. Yeah, she was going to drift off soon. I tried to resist the temptation to make faces at her and failed completely. I could have spent the time making those notes Bernie wanted but... well, screw that.

When Jan arrived, I popped an Ativan, said hello, put on my winter gear, and left the house. I wanted to talk to Hal Buckwald, but I had no idea where he lived. My Nana Cole probably knew, but the atmosphere in that kitchen had turned arctic and I'd just wanted to get out of there.

Speaking of arctic, the moment I walked out the back door I was slapped in the face by the frigid air. It had to be well below ten degrees. That made up my mind. I took the Escalade. The plow had come through again and dumped almost of a foot of snow at the end of the driveway. For the

SUV, driving through it wasn't a problem. Like driving over a dead body.

Anyway, I figured the best way to find Hal would be to ask his cousin Buford. I'd pretty much figured out where the Campbell—compound? complex? nuclear test site?—was located, so I pointed myself in that direction and about fifteen minutes later I was at Buford's door.

As I stood there waiting for him to come to the door, I noticed that the wind had blown away some snow and there was what looked like a green plaid blanket beneath the snow. *What was that about?* I wondered just as he opened the door.

"Hi. Me again."

This time, he cracked it open a little wider. I took that to mean we were becoming friends. He wore stained long underwear and had a bad case of bedhead. I found myself saying, "I'm sorry I woke you."

"I wasn't asleep. I've been awake since 1993."

Couldn't possibly be true, but I got the point.

"Well, I'm sorry to bother you. I'm looking for Hal Buckwald. Bobbie's son. I thought you might know where he lives."

Without another word, he wove an arm out the door, pointing at the mobile home in the back of the lot, the one with no siding, then closed the door. Okay, well, that was an answer.

I picked my way out to the trailer using other people's footsteps. As nearly as I could tell, no one had shoveled a path to the trailer. There were multiple sets of footsteps through the recent snow leading to and from its front door.

I banged on the storm door. A few moments later, Hal opened the door. He, too, was wearing long underwear. He did have a pair of jeans covering the bottom part, which I appreciated.

"Hi, we haven't met, I'm Henry Milch. I'm wondering if I could ask a few questions about your mother?"

"Are you with the newspaper?"

"No, no I'm not. You know it's awfully cold out here, I wonder if I could come inside—"

"No, you can't."

I suppose that was a blessing. From what I could see the interior of the mobile home looked like a picked-over yard sale, and there was a disturbing smell wafting out. Then again... frostbite.

"I've heard you didn't get on with your mother. Is that true?"

"Nobody got on with my mother. Not for long. Is there a reward? Is that why you're nosing around?"

"When was the last time you spoke to her?"

"About a year ago. If you get a reward, I want part of it."

"There's no reward. Don't you care who killed your mother?"

"Not really."

That brought me to a halt. I mean, if someone killed my mother, I'd want to know who it was. Finally, I asked, "What's the deal with this... property? Why are you all living on it?"

He looked me up and down, seeming to decide whether he wanted to answer. "So, my great-great grandfather Malcolm Campbell, Scottish, got a land grant for a hundred and sixty acres. He was going to be a farmer, but he wasn't great at it. Ended up selling off most of the trees for lumber. He died and left the land to his two sons. They weren't much better at farming, and ended up selling off a lot of the land during the Depression. By the time my grandfather and his two cousins inherited the land there wasn't much left. Just four and a half acres."

"How many people own this property now?"

"Five cousins."

"So, you've been living on the same piece of property as your mom. How did you not speak to her for a whole year?"

"Easier than you think. She was always trying to borrow money. I finally told her to fuck off. She did."

"What did she want to borrow money for?"

He raised an eyebrow at me. "Doctor visit. Blinski."

That did not need explaining. What did need explaining was why she thought her son would have any money to loan her. He certainly didn't look like he had any.

He went on, "By the time I told her to fuck off she owed me about twelve hundred dollars. I knew I'd never see it again."

"The night your mother died, did you see anyone on the property?"

"I already talked to a deputy. They know I didn't see anything." I thought he'd finished, but then he went on. "Two of my cousins live in the other singlewide. I was over there with them most of the night."

"What were you doing?"

"Terminator."

"Watching the movie?"

"No, the game." Then he said, "I'll be back" in a bad imitation for Arnold Schwarzenegger's Austrian accent.

"What time did you get back here?"

"Four, five."

He could have easily killed his mother and then driven over and dumped her body at Three Friends well before the sun came up.

"What kind of car do you drive?"

"I didn't kill my mother. If I was going to kill her, I'd have done it a long, long time ago."

Then he shut the door in my face.

As I was leaving, I wondered what time Bobbie was killed. I got into the SUV and turned the heat up to high. Then I sat there doing math in my head. Don't laugh, it's possible.

Melanie was seen at Roberta's around one in the morning. If she was the killer, she'd have to have carried the body to her car, and then driven to the winery and dumped it. If Hal were the killer, his alibi went until sometime between four and five. He could have killed her at five and then gotten the body over to Three Friends by five-thirty. My obsessive viewing of *CSI* had taught me that time of death was determined by body temperature. At some point after I left the crime scene, the medical examiner showed up and stuck a thermometer directly into Roberta's liver (gross, I know), and took her internal temperature.

So if Roberta was killed around one in the morning and her temperature was taken at, say, ten o'clock, that was nine hours. But, if she was killed at five-thirty or six, that would be only two or two and a half hours.

Leaving a body out in the cold would drop its temperature quickly. Normal body temperature is 98.6, round that up to a hundred. If the body loses four degrees per hour, the body's temperature would be around fifty-five degrees if Melanie was the killer. On the other hand, if Hal was the killer the body's temperature would be closer to eighty-five.

Wait, was that right? I ran the numbers in my head again. Yup, that was right. So...did Detective Lehmann already have the autopsy report? Did he know Roberta's time of death? Is that why he hadn't already arrested Melanie? Was Roberta killed much later than Melanie's visit?

I got out my flip phone and called Ham. When he answered it was obvious he was outside again. I couldn't help but ask, "Why are you always outside? It's winter?"

"I've got this workman's comp case, and the guy keeps coming to the park. It's kind of a cruising spot. I've watched him pick up a couple guys. Usually, he gets a blow job in his car."

"Is this the same guy who was doing triple axels?"

"I have more than one case."

"Are they always outside?"

Actually, when I thought about it, the case he'd given me had led to my being outside a lot more than I wanted to be.

Ignoring me, he said, "I need to catch him doing something strenuous. Getting a blow job doesn't cut it."

"Maybe he's really injured."

"Yeah, that happens. Not often, but it happens. What are you calling about?"

"When do you think we'll get the autopsy for Roberta LaCross?"

"Possibly never. We'll have to wait for Melanie to be arrested and arraigned. Discovery should happen shortly after that. It doesn't always though, and a medical examiner can always hold the report pending review."

"Is there a way to find out now?"

"We'd need a member of the family to request it."

I thought about that. We'd have to pay Hal... and he was

kind of a suspect. Maybe Buford would ask? Or another Campbell?

"Why are you so curious?" Ham asked.

I explained my theory about time of death. In the middle of my explanation I got another call, but I let it go to voicemail. When I was done, Ham said, "You're probably right that the time of death excludes Melanie. Lehmann is probably looking for some kind of evidence that she came back later. Do you have any idea what direction their investigation is taking?"

"I think they're mainly harassing me."

"How did things go with Bernie Schaub?"

I told him everything that had happened that morning. Apparently, they'd already talked because he said, "When you finish that report he asked for, make sure to email me a copy. Okay?"

That was annoying. I'd carefully avoided mentioning the report. Now it seemed like I might actually have to write it. Crap. The last thing I wanted this job to be about was writing reports.

I said goodbye, then checked my messages. Opal, sounding desperate. When I called back, I'd barely said hello when she said, "Denny is missing."

"Yeah, well, drug addicts do that."

I could have offered up myself as proof but decided not to. She really didn't need to know I'd fallen off the map once for four days. I might have gone to Vegas or maybe a poker club in Gardena, that part is fuzzy. Anyway, I was trying to pay attention to the conversation, but mostly what she was saying was, "Carl is frantic." "Carl is terrified." "Carl is heartbroken."

"How long has Denny been gone?"

"Two days."

"Look, he's probably off partying and having sex with someone and will be for another day or so."

Denny and I had vastly different tastes in drugs. I liked the kind that offered bliss and a long nap. He preferred the ones that compelled you to have so much sex you rubbed off patches of skin in your nether regions.

"He'll come back when he's ready," I said, trying to sound reassuring. "Or when he runs out of drugs."

"Can you go to a meeting? Someone there might know where Denny is."

"It's not Thursday."

"There are other people in the world besides gays."

"Yes, far too many."

"You have to help, Henry."

For the life of me I couldn't figure out why I had to help. We were frenemies at best. That implied I didn't owe her a thing.

"Fine. I've got an idea. I'll call you back."

I clicked off wondering what was wrong with me? Why had I agreed to help her? This was not going to end well.

I drove to the Turley HIV clinic, which was located in a small brick building a block or so from the HealthWeb Hospital, which was previously... Okay, you get the picture. I almost couldn't find it. It sat next to one of the overflow parking lots for the hospital, which was also where they kept their overflow snow. Next to the tiny building was a two-story mountain of dirty snow.

I drove around looking for a parking space that didn't have a meter and then walked the four blocks to the clinic. Of course, the place was empty. Sexually transmitted diseases seemed more a summer thing. You might be bored enough to contract them in the winter, but no one would notice them until summertime.

Todd sat at a desk in one corner. There was a plaque with his full name: TODDY MILNER. I kept running into him, so maybe I should make an effort to remember his name. Nah, whatever. He looked up and saw me.

"Hello. Nice to see you. Are you here for an HIV test?"

"No. God no. I might as well be a nun. Pickings up here are pretty slim."

"I don't know that I agree with that. You might have to dig a little deeper than you would in Los Angeles. Maybe don't be so picky."

What a thing to say to a person. I prided myself on my pickiness. I mean, fine, I'll admit that when I was in search of Oxy I wasn't always picky. But sober, sober I was very picky.

"Actually, I came to see you."

"Oh, that's great! You considered my offer? I'm off in about forty-five minutes. We could have a cup of coffee and talk about what it means to have a sponsor."

"Oh no, no that's not what I meant. Not at all." I stared at his confused face for a moment, then rushed forward, "I'm friends with Opal who works at Pastiche."

"I know Opal."

"Well, she's friends with Carl, who's friends... well, he has a thing for Denny."

"Yes, I'm familiar."

"Great. Denny is missing and Carl is freaking out, which means Opal is freaking out and she's calling me to help find Denny. Do you have any idea where he might be?"

"Okay. Hmmm... You remember the anonymous part, right?"

"So he has been coming to meetings," I guessed. I mean, there wouldn't be anything to keep anonymous if he wasn't, right? That was great. I had a least one thing to tell Opal.

Toddy seemed to be thinking the situation over. Then he asked, "How long has he been missing?"

"A couple of days."

"There's a chat room on AOL. M-4-M-P-N-P, you could check there. You might not get an honest answer, though. You could check Craigslist M4M, go back a few days and see if anyone was looking for PNP. You might find something there."

I had no intention of doing these things myself, I would

pass them onto Opal. She or Carl could snoop around online. I did a lot online, but finding tweakers on a bender was not a precedent I wanted to set.

"And, of course, Ronnie Scheck might have some idea."

That was a little more challenging. Opal would definitely want me to go and talk to him. I might not mention that possibility.

"So, Henry, tell me how you got addicted to OxyContin."

"Why would I do that?"

"Because you can't solve a problem until you admit you have one. Tell me how your problem started?"

I didn't want to answer that, it really wasn't any of his business, but I found myself saying, "My stepfather pushed me down the stairs when I was fourteen. He told everyone I did it to myself. That I was trying to kill myself."

"And that led to your taking Oxy?"

I nodded.

"Were you hurt badly?"

"I broke my wrist. My back was messed up for a while."

"And you didn't tell your doctor when it got better? You just kept getting prescriptions?"

I shrugged.

"So you've been an addict for nine, ten years?"

"No. I basically stopped right before college. And I was... sober, I guess, for most of the four years I was in college."

"And afterwards?"

I shrugged. "I hadn't forgotten what it was like. I kind of missed it. And by then I was going out to bars, and someone would buy me a drink. It wasn't hard to ask if they knew where I could get some Oxy. You know, this is none of your business."

He smiled knowingly. "Yes, I remember that. The idea that my addiction was no one's business but my own. You get over that."

That's what he thought.

THE NEXT MORNING, I had the dream again. I hadn't had it in years. Falling. That's how it always started. The feeling of falling through space. It wasn't pleasant; it wasn't what an astronaut or a skydiver might feel. I knew I would land, and the landing wouldn't be soft. Sometimes I would wake up just then... The fear of landing wrapped around me like a shawl.

Worse though were the mornings I didn't wake up. The mornings I landed. Pain shot through me. A bone cracked. White light that wasn't light flashing across my vision. When my eyes cleared, if they cleared—it was a dream after all—when they cleared, I could see I was at the bottom of a staircase. At the top of the stairs, my stepfather, Frank Fetterman, was staring down at me, smiling, sometimes giggling. Always pleased with himself. It was a dream, but it was also a memory.

I shouldn't have talked about falling down the stairs with Toddy. There were things I shouldn't talk about, shouldn't think about. This was one of them.

I tried to roll over, but Riley was asleep on my legs like a seventy-pound blanket. It was still dark, but that didn't mean much. At this time of year, it was dark until almost 9 a.m. My guess was it was before six. Emerald hadn't woken yet. In just a little while she'd get restless, and I'd go down the hall and pick her up. I'd change her, then bring her downstairs and make a bottle for her. I'd try another mashed banana and some rice cereal.

I wondered if my mother was ever coming back. If past was prologue, she would be back. Once things were a little easier. I have to be honest and admit there are definitely worse people than my mother—and she had a habit of attracting them. By comparison, she often looked good. I don't think she did it on purpose. Yes, she was manipulative, but choosing people who were bad enough to make her look good was genius level manipulation. And I don't think she's a genius. She's just unlucky in lucky ways. That's all.

Down the hall, Emerald let out an exploratory cry. The day was beginning. As I changed her, I wondered about what I should try to accomplish. I had a report to write, which meant I had to do things that allowed me to ignore that. Important things that would allow me to say, I couldn't possibly write up that report, I was doing the important thing. I just had no idea what that was.

The truth was, there wasn't much to do. It was looking more and more like our client, Melanie Frasier, was in the clear. She hadn't been arrested. They clearly didn't have enough evidence against her. If this were *Law & Order*, Melanie would be suspect number one, at fifteen minutes we'd learn that she couldn't possibly have done it, and after the commercial break, we'd move on to another suspect—also not the killer. The killer was never discovered until the forty-five-minute mark, leading to a long and dramatic confession, a few ironic remarks from the detectives and a lot more commercials.

When Emerald and I arrived in the kitchen, Nana Cole was already sitting at the table with a cup of tea in front of her. I said, "Good morning" but got no response.

I got Emerald into the high chair, and she immediately began to bang the tray, as though demanding her breakfast. I put a saucepan on the stove with some water and turned it on so I could warm up her bottle. Then I mashed up a banana in a bowl. While I waited for the water to warm, I sat across from Emerald and stuck a spoon full of banana into her mouth.

"Are you not talking to me?" I asked Nana Cole without turning around to look at her.

Silence was my answer. I ignored her for a long time. Once I'd heated up the formula, I used a bit of it to make the rice cereal, and tried to figure out which to give her first. The food thing was still new. Should I do one after the other or should I intersperse them? Adults, most adults, like to have some liquid with their meal and food: liquid, food, liquid. Did babies do the same? I decided to follow our pediatrician's advice and let Emerald lead. I got some cereal into her, some banana, and then offered her the bottle. She took it.

That left me wondering how to get it away from her. Should I coax it away or just let her finish. I decided to wait for disinterest. While I waited, I made my grandmother a simple breakfast. Most mornings she didn't have much more than an apple and some peanut butter. Occasionally, she might have toast or an English muffin. Once in a while, some scrambled eggs.

I cut up the apple, smeared a coupled of tablespoons of peanut butter onto the plate and set it in front of her.

"If you want something else, just say so."

I sat back down across from Emerald again. I really wanted to make a pot of coffee, but that would have to wait. My sister had lost interest in the bottle and plunked a hand into cereal bowl, mushing the contents between her fingers. I took her spoon and scraped some of it off her hands and put it into her mouth. She looked uncertain but kept moving it around her mouth.

Behind me, Nana Cole said, "This is all your fault."

I was pretty sure I knew what she meant, but said, "Babies are messy. I'm sure I've heard you say that a few times."

"Everything's different since you got here."

"That doesn't make anything my fault."

"I think it does. I haven't figured out how, yet. But I will."

This was a particular kind of thinking I was familiar with, though she hadn't applied it to me before. Whenever something happened that she didn't like—the cost of Medicare going up, groceries prices rising, a pothole in Masons Bay, whatever—it was always the Democrats' fault. She could seldom explain why—until she'd watched Sean Hannity, though even then the explanations were shaky. She knew who she wanted to blame and blamed them. Logic be damned.

"Your friends didn't catch lesbianism from me, if that's what you think."

I kept my focus on Emerald. I wasn't entirely sure she wasn't about to throw both of us into the street. Everything she believed would be telling her that's the right thing to do. I regretted not having my convertible roof fixed. I suppose if I just filled the car up and drove south we'd be in warmer weather in a day or so. Maybe it wasn't such a disaster. Though couch surfing in Los Angeles would be a lot more difficult with a baby in tow. I'd need to get a job pretty quickly. One where I could bring the baby with me. I certainly couldn't afford daycare. I didn't even want to think about how little there was left in my bank account. Of course, I could take Nana Cole's credit card with me. It would take her a few days to cancel it.

Jesus Christ, how did women do this?

And then, I heard the crunch of Nana Cole biting into her apple. This was how we Coles did things. We moved forward, usually vowing to ignore whatever the problem was. Apologies were not offered, lessons were not learned, secrets became things that never happened. It's not a bad coping mechanism, particularly since I didn't want to end up floating around the country in a leaky convertible with an infant.

"I played trivia with Patty Gauthier and Brian Belcher the other night. Do you know much about them?"

After a moment, she said, "I know they live next door to each other. Patty was married once long time ago. Sheriff Crocker's cousin, I think. No one thought it would last. She didn't even take his name. Wouldn't commit. The Belcher boy lost his mother long time ago, then his father last winter sometime. Cancer, both of them, I think. I'm surprised he's still around. Most younger people would sell the house and move on. Summer people are paying a lot for houses on the water."

"Patty told me Bobbie LaCross killed a man. Did you ever hear that?"

I still wasn't looking at her. Wasn't sure that was a good idea. Our truce was delicate and newborn; I didn't want to ruin it. Besides, Emerald was doing an excellent job on her breakfast.

"No, I never heard anything like that."

And then, I put two and two together.

"Oh shit."

"Watch your mouth in front of the baby."

"Yes ma'am."

Oh shit! I just remembered more about meeting Bobbie outside Ronnie Sheck's trailer. She told a story about a man with cancer giving her Oxy. She flirted with him, so he gave her the pills. That man was Brian Belcher's father. It had to mean something.

But what?

CHAPTER SIXTEEN

Around ten-thirty I called Opal. It was a choice between calling her and doing the paperwork I'd been asked to do. She was clearly the lesser of two evils.

"Did Denny come back?" I asked when she picked up.

"No. What have you done to find him?"

"Wait. Do you think you hired me?"

"Why would I hire you?"

"Why would I do anything if you haven't hired me?"

"Because you're a friend."

"*Am* I a friend?"

"You call me for rides like I'm your friend."

"I have a car."

"For now."

I heard a bell in the background and Opal said, "Good morning. Welcome to Pastiche." She was working. Good. Maybe they'd buy something, and she'd have to hang up.

A moment later, she said to me, "Where were we?"

It took a great deal of self-control not to say 'You were being a bitch.' Instead, I said, "Okay, fine, I did talk to someone about how tweakers hook up. You might want to go to Craigslist, back to the last time you knew where Denny was, and check out who was looking for PNP. You could pretend to want to hook up and ask about Denny."

"I can't do that. I'm a girl."

"They won't know that."

"They'll ask for a picture."

"Take a shirtless picture of Carl and send that."

She got quiet, and I worried for a moment if I'd sent her into a sexual frenzy just thinking about a sexy photoshoot with Carl. Then she said, "If Denny's still there with them doing... whatever, then they're not going to respond."

That was a good point. Meanwhile, her customer asked, "Is this the only color you have?" I imagined the woman was holding up a blouse or something.

"It is..." Opal said with a mix of regret and loathing. Then back to me, "Could you go talk to Ronnie Scheck for me?"

"Why can't you go?"

"I'm not a customer of his. He's not going to talk to me."

"I'm not a customer of his anymore."

The ensuing silence was damning and a tiny bit deserved.

"Fine. Okay, I'll try to fit it in. It might take a day or two."

"You can't be that busy."

"I happen to be investigating Bobbie LaCross's murder." Okay, that was an overstatement but at least close to the truth.

Then she said, "You don't know? Patty Gauthier confessed this morning."

"How do you know that?"

"My first two customers told me all about it."

That prompted her current customer to say, "I heard that too. Apparently, she stabbed Bobbie thirty-six times."

"Bobbie was strangled," Opal and I said at the same time.

"Well, that's just what I heard," the customer said.

I said good-bye, though why I bothered I do not know.

Patty confessed? Why would she do that? Yes, they had issues. But Patty had gotten rid of her. She no longer lived at Patty's house. She was just an annoying person she occasionally ran into. That wasn't a good reason to kill someone. Not that there *are* good reasons to kill people, but some reasons are better than others and this was definitely not a better reason.

I was about to go downstairs and tell my grandmother she'd missed an opportunity to gossip, when my phone rang. It was Bernie Schaub, Jr.

"I don't know if you've heard—" he began.

"I have."

"Yes, well, I'm taking my aunt's case and I'll need an investigator. Can I hire you directly? What's your hourly?"

That was a problem. For one, I didn't know my hourly. I kept forgetting to ask. And for two, I worked for Hamlet. We never talked about this kind of situation, but it didn't feel, well, ethical.

"You know, I should probably talk to Ham first."

"Interesting. After everything I've heard about you, I thought you'd jump at the chance."

"What have you heard about me?"

"That you're a drug addict, very slutty and passably clever."

"Well, you heard wrong. I'm passably slutty and very clever. Actually, I think I only had sex once last year."

"Well, in Masons Bay once is enough to get you called a slut."

I really needed to change the direction of this conversation. "I'm very happy to work for you. You should probably book me through Hamlet, though."

"Oh, very well. I'll call him later this afternoon. Consider yourself hired."

"So, you don't think your aunt did it?"

"I have no idea. She says she did so she probably did."

"But she's your aunt."

"Oh, I lost all faith in humanity right after puberty."

Honestly, he didn't look like he'd *finished* puberty.

"So, I think Bobbie was killed at the Campbell compound

and then thrown in front of Three Friends Winery. Do you think your aunt is strong enough to strangle a seventy-year-old woman and then carry her to a car, in the snow, and then dump her somewhere else?"

"I have no idea. The sheriff is going to have to prove that, isn't he?"

And I figured that was where we'd start. When Jan arrived at noon, I ran out of the house and drove to the Municipal Center. It was a beautiful day. When the sky is a clear blue and the snow a sparkling white and the temperature in the high twenties, I can almost appreciate winter. Almost.

I was in the Metro, so I slid into a parking place and then went into the sheriff's office. Bernie had asked me to meet him there so we could talk to his aunt together. On the way, I'd called Hamlet and explained Bernie's offer.

He said, "Thank you for being ethical. And bringing in work. I think you've earned yourself a two dollar an hour increase.

"Which brings me to... how much?"

"Oh shit! I've got to go."

I would have thought he was faking if it weren't for the gunfire in the background.

Anyway, I reached the sheriff's office before Bernie. I stopped the moment I walked in. The office was basically a large, communal room with a lot of empty desks. The room was ringed by offices and interview rooms. In my other visits it had been a deadly quiet place. Today, though, it was noisy and chaotic.

Several of the deputies were there standing with Detective Lehmann, as they watched Patty Gauthier attempting to carry Lehmann's wife Gloria around the room. Gloria was a very attractive, petite blond who was likely around Bobbie's weight. Detective Lehmann had devised a way for Patty to prove her confession true.

Gloria lay over Patty's shoulders in what looked like a fireman's carry.

"Honey, relax, you're a corpse," Detective Lehman said from the sidelines.

"I'm trying."

Patty was struggling a bit, but she was managing it.

"Really, Rudy, I could have written you an equation that would have proven whether this was physically possible or not," Gloria said. She taught algebra.

And then, Bernie Schaub, Jr. was behind me saying, "Oh no, no, no, no-no-no."

"I'm just verifying Patty's confession," Detective Lehmann said.

"Bernie, you don't need to be here," Patty said as she put Gloria down. She wiped some sweat off her forehead. "I've confessed. I don't need an attorney."

"Aunt Patty, that's when you need an attorney the most." He looked at Detective Lehmann and said, "Manslaughter."

"She's already confessed that she went to Bobbie's home with the intention of killing her."

Bernie looked at his aunt, and said, "You really should have talked to me first."

"I just wanted to get it over with."

Detective Lehmann said, "Why don't you and your client go into an interview room. We'll get a search warrant for her home... Unless you'd like to give us permission?"

"Yes, go ahead," Patty said.

"Uh-no... get a warrant."

"We'll get a warrant."

Then we went into the interview room. Bernie nodded in my direction, indicating that I should join them. Once in the room, there were only two chairs, so I leaned up against the wall. I was, of course, the least important person there.

"I just can't believe this. Aunt Patty, how could you do something this horrible?"

"Well, Bobbie took advantage of me for a very long time and I just reached—"

"No, I don't mean murder. I mean, how could you confess? You must have some idea how inept the sheriff's office is. They'd never have figured out the killer was you. What possessed you?"

"Well... actually, it was you..." She was looking right at me.

"Me? What did I do?"

"You were asking all those questions at trivia night. I just had the feeling you'd figure it out eventually. So, I confessed."

Bernie glared at me for a moment. I thought he might fire me on the spot. He turned back to his aunt, and said, "Tell us everything that happened the night of the murder."

"Well, I knew Patty went to Main Street Café most nights. I waited until around two, two-thirty in the morning, and then I drove over to the Campbell compound. I turned off my lights a couple houses away. Left my car out on the road and walked up the driveway."

"Was Patty's car there?" I asked. I knew it hadn't been so if she said...

"No, it wasn't there."

"But you thought Patty would be?"

"When she lived with me, I'd have to drive her into Masons Bay to get her car in the mornings. I knew what she was like." She took a deep breath and continued. "I walked up the driveway to the RV she was living in, I opened the door and went in—"

Shaking my head, I said, "The door was unlocked. Oh my god, when are people up here going to learn?"

Ignoring me, Bernie asked, "You're in the trailer. What happened?"

"I strangled her."

"While she was laying down? Did she get up? Was she asleep?" Bernie shot questions at her.

"Stop, please." Patty steadied herself. "Bobbie was drunk...

and she may have taken something. She did that, a lot when she lived with me. She'd mix alcohol and OxyContin. She didn't wake up. While I was strangling her, she didn't wake up."

"Could she have been dead already?" Bernie asked. I was glad he asked that and not me. The whole thing was making me uncomfortable.

"I don't know. It's possible. I didn't check to see if she was alive before I killed her."

"Pity. It might have saved a lot of trouble." Bernie frowned obviously unhappy with the whole thing. Then, "Never mind. The autopsy should tell us if she was already dead. And even if it doesn't... Were you wearing gloves?"

"Yes. I didn't bother to take them off."

"Why didn't you use a pillow?" I asked, trying to make myself useful.

Patty looked confused for a moment. Lehmann must not have asked her this. Then she said, "It's an RV. Getting around was awkward. But I'm not sure I thought about it at the time."

"And then you carried her to your car?" Bernie asked.

"I tried to carry her. And did, for a bit. I also dragged her part of the way."

"And then?"

"I put her in my trunk. Drove to Three Friends. And then rolled her down the slope to the front door."

Having been there later that morning, I had a very clear visual of Bobbie's body, making me ask. "What about the parka? When did you put it onto her?"

"She was wearing it."

"She was wearing the parka in bed?"

"Yes."

"Excellent," Bernie said.

"Why, why is that excellent?" I asked.

"She passed out before taking her coat off. It suggests she

was heavily drugged. It supports the idea she was already dead."

I thought that a bit of a stretch, but he might sell it to a jury. I tried to think back, did anything Melanie say contradict this? I didn't think it did, but she was going to have to give a detailed statement to the police. I did have one question though...

"You told me Bobbie killed a man down in Detroit. I think you were lying."

She sighed, heavily, and said, "That has nothing to do with this."

Which convinced me it did.

CHAPTER SEVENTEEN

After we finished our interview with Patty, Bernie went and talked privately with Detective Lehmann. Alone. That was annoying. Honestly, I didn't understand why I didn't get to join them. The general area outside the offices was now empty, the deputies and Gloria Lehmann were gone.

I took a moment to call Hamlet with an update. When he picked up, I asked, "Are you okay? When I talked to you earlier, I heard shots.

"Oh, don't worry about that. No one was shooting at me. Of course, I'm a lot less interested in marriage now." Moving on quickly, he asked, "Weren't you supposed to send me a report and an invoice?"

That was completely true. I tried to sidestep it. "Not since the last time we talked." I mean, I never sent one, but if I had it wouldn't need updating from the last few hours. Although, actually it would...

"Bernie is really upset that his aunt confessed, though she's adamant."

"She was at Three Friends when Bobbie took her fall. Right?"

"And then Bobbie mooched off her for, like, nine months."

"Is she saying why she decided to kill Bobbie *now*?"

"Not really. And..."

"And what?"

"Patty says she strangled Bobbie while she was asleep. But... I saw Bobbie's face after she died. She looked terrified, like she knew exactly what was happening."

After a moment, he said, "Did you tell that to Bernie?"

"Not yet."

"Keep it to yourself for now. We'll see how things develop. Good job, though."

"Speaking of which, we need to talk about how much—"

Lehmann's door opened and Bernie came out. I said to Ham, "Gotta go." And clicked off the call.

When he reached me, Bernie said, "They've got a search warrant coming in half an hour. I want you to go out to Aunt Patty's house and be there while it's searched. I would do it but, a) it's going to be super boring, and b) I have to get Aunt Patty bail. Not going to be easy. You've been to the house, you remember where it is?"

"I do."

"Make sure they give you a receipt for everything they take. Also, read the warrant and make sure they don't take anything that isn't specifically listed."

"Is it going to take long? I can only be there until four-thirty."

He frowned at me. "I don't know how long it's going to take. It depends on whether they drag their feet or not."

Then he stared at me until I said, "If they run late, I'll try to get a babysitter."

He looked a bit confused by that statement. I decided not to explain since he'd managed to find out I was a drug addict and arguably a slut. If he couldn't figure out I was taking care of my baby sister that was his problem.

"You'd better get going. I don't want them there without you."

I did manage to make it there before the deputies arrived. Which meant I was standing in the open doorway—yes, the front door was unlocked—when deputy Twiss and his two buddies got out of a black SUV and walked up to the door.

"What the fuck are you doing here?" Twiss asked.

"Can I see the search warrant?" I said, holding out my hand.

"Are you related to Patty Gauthier?"

"I'm on her legal team."

Begrudgingly, Twiss handed me the warrant which was covered in a blue sheet of paper. "Now get out of our way before I arrest you."

I stepped aside and let them into the house. Honestly, being arrested was not one of my favorite things. After they entered the house, I closed the front door and stood in the mudroom reading the warrant. The date, Patty's name, the address, legalese, legalese, legalese, then the areas they could search: the house, garages, outbuildings, the grounds and any vehicles. That was pretty comprehensive. More legalese. Then, the items they could take: gloves and other winter outer-wear, items originally belonging to Roberta LaCross, diaries, day planners, calendars, home videos, photograph albums, bank records, phone records, computers, answering machines and cell phones. That was also a pretty extensive list. I wondered if they should have brought a U-Haul.

I hadn't had any time to really look around. This part of the house was a great room, a large open space that included a kitchen with a gigantic island, the living room area which was defined by a gray sectional that would have taken up three rooms in my grandmother's house, a dining area and a fireplace with a couple of comfortable looking chairs in front of it.

Beyond all that was a wall of three French doors opening onto an expansive wooden deck, now dormant and covered in nearly a foot of snow. Lake Michigan was beyond all that, calm for the moment, gray like sky.

The décor was beach house despite Patty's being a local: whitewashed, distressed furniture struggling to look cast off from a grand city home, a general overwrought casualness defined by a plaque in the kitchen that read IT'S WINE O'CLOCK SOMEWHERE.

The deputies were all within sight. One only a few feet from me going through the coats hanging from hooks on the wall. I was still near the front door, in what some would call a foyer but in Michigan was definitely a mudroom.

The deputy had found a pair of winter gloves and was putting them into a plastic bag.

"I'd like to take a photo of those, if you don't mind."

He studied me suspiciously and then brought the evidence bag over to the sectional. "I'll set things here and you can photo them. Don't touch anything."

I got out my nifty Samsung flip phone and took a not-very-good photo of the gloves. They were winter gloves, so I doubted very much Patty wore them to strangle Bobbie. They were fleece-lined suede. The kind of winter gloves that made most tasks, including the strangling of seventy-year-old women, almost impossible.

The other deputies picked up on the procedure and as their bagged "evidence" appeared on the sofa, I took a photo of it. There were more gloves, a couple of scarfs, a Day Runner for 2003, a small wall calendar (2004) from the kitchen. I took photos of all of it until I got a message on my Samsung's tiny screen that I'd run out of memory.

I had taken a bunch of photos of Riley and Emerald that I should have moved to my iBook, but I needed a special adapter. I just hadn't gotten around to picking one up. If I was going to keep working for Ham, I'd probably need to do that. In the meantime, I had to delete photos I didn't want to, but I had Reilly, and I had Emerald. I could take more photos as soon as I got my cell phone cleared out. I spent a good ten minutes navigating the phone's menu and repeatedly pressing delete.

The most fruitful item they found, in my estimation, was a cardboard box filled with things Bobbie had left behind when she moved out. There was a sling she must have used when she broke her arm, a wrist brace presumably from when she snapped her wrist, three Sudoku books mostly complete, a pair of reading glasses from a drug store, a huge, empty prescription bottle made out to Roberta LaCross for lorazepam, a smaller prescription bottle made out to Russell Belcher, also empty, for hydrocodone—which was basically Oxy.

This proved my idea that Bobbie's story about getting Oxy from a man with cancer was true, and that man was Brian Belcher's father. So was this what Patty meant when she said Bobbie killed a man once? That she'd killed Russell Belcher? No, that didn't make sense. Taking his Oxy wouldn't have killed him. He might have been left in unbearable pain, but people didn't die of unbearable pain—did they?

"How much longer do you think you'll be?" I asked Twiss as he lay a plastic bag containing a daily calendar from 1999 onto the sofa. Pointless if you ask me.

"Don't know. You got to be some place?"

As a matter of fact, I did. I went back to the mudroom and called Jan to see if she could stay late. She couldn't, she had a ceramics class she didn't want to miss. Then I called Dorothy to see if she could babysit. She could not. That left one possibility, one my Nana Cole would hate.

"Hi, Bev. It's Henry. How are you?"

"Well, upset, of course."

"Yes. Of course you are. You really can't take the things she says seriously, though..."

"Henry, I've known Emma since before you were born."

She had me there; I had to turn that to my advantage.

"Then you know that what she's best at is denial."

Okay, fine, it's a family trait. Get over yourself.

"What are you saying?"

"I need help. With Emerald. I'm stuck on a job-related thing..." I was trying to be discreet, but then I realized a bit of gossip would help Bev smooth things over with Nana Cole. "Patty Gauthier confessed to murdering Bobbie LaCross. I have to stay at Patty's house while they search it. Nana Cole doesn't know yet, if you could just go over, act like nothing happened, and tell her what's going on... you'll probably be fine."

"Or she'll throw us out."

"If she does, take the baby to your place."

"And she'll have us arrested us for kidnapping."

Really, getting a babysitter should not be this hard.

"I'm asking you to, so it's not kidnapping."

"Are you Emerald's guardian?"

"No. But neither is Nana Cole. My mother is Emerald's guardian."

We were in a very gray area. I could almost hear Bev thinking that if my grandmother called the police, the baby might get taken away by child protective services. A judge might grant one of us custody, but I certainly didn't want to go up against a well-informed social worker.

"All right," Bev said. "We'll call you if it doesn't go well."

I wanted to suggest she not bring Barbara, but they seemed to only travel as a pair. I wasn't sure if that was because of their lesbianism, their age, or if it was simply unique to them. Whatever it was, I found it very strange. I'd met few men I could tolerate all the way through the sex act (without Oxy, I mean) so the idea of being with anyone in that way twenty-four-seven was deeply disturbing.

After I hung up, I noticed that my phone was nearly out of a charge. The charger was at home in my bedroom. I really hoped Bev and Barbara didn't need to talk to me since they might not get through. I might need a better phone if I was going to keep working for Ham. I wonder if he'd let me expense that? Could I expense things? I really needed to ask—

Someone was knocking at the door, so I went over and answered it. It was Brian Belcher from next door. He had a worried look on his face.

"What's going on? Why is the sheriff here? Is Patty all right?"

"They're searching the house. Patty confessed to murder this morning."

"Wait—what? Patty confessed to killing Bobbie?"

"I just said that."

"Is she okay? Does she need a lawyer?"

"Her nephew is taking her case."

"Bernie, junior. Okay."

He still looked very concerned. His forehead was creased and his jaw tight.

"I'd invite you in, but I don't think they'd like it."

"It's all right. I should—"

As he began to walk away, I stepped out onto the stoop and asked, "Were Patty and your dad close?"

Turning around, he said, "Oh, um, yeah. They were friendly."

"Bobbie used to get painkillers from your dad, didn't she?"

"How do you know that?"

"It's just something I heard."

"He liked her, that's all. He thought she was fun. Some people did."

"Do you think it contributed to his death? Could it have hastened the cancer in some way?"

He went still for a moment, then said, "He died of a heart attack. He had medicine, but he couldn't get to it in time."

That was odd, I hadn't expected it. Did it mean something? I was about to ask more questions, but Brian said, "Look, I have to go. I've got things I need to do."

He walked part way down the short driveway, around the

far side of the sheriff's SUV. I expected to see him walking the way out to the road and then back up his driveway, which was obscured by trees, but he didn't reappear. That was strange. Had he fallen down? Was he hiding? What was happening?

I walked over to the SUV, then around... I found a neatly shoveled path through the trees which connected the Belcher property to Patty's. I hadn't noticed it before. I mean, come on, everything was white. But now that I did see it, I wondered, why? Why take the time to shovel a path between the houses? The end of the driveway was only another twenty feet. They couldn't have been going from house to house that often. Could they? And why...

Oh crap. There was something going on between Patty and Brian. I'd seen them together at Trivia. She was all dolled up. I guess I hadn't picked up on it, since she was older than he was by... fifteen years? Possibly less. To cut myself some slack, I was taking care of a baby that night. And playing trivia. And asking a lot of *other* questions. Plus... who really understands the things straight people do?

Anyway, now that I figured it out, what did it mean? Did it mean anything? I kind of remembered that Russell Belcher died about a year ago. So it was an anniversary. Patty killed Bobbie on the anniversary of her lover's father's death. No, that didn't make much sense. So what did make sense?

I realized I was freezing my ass off, so I went back inside.

They finished up around six. I was starving and cursing the fact that the nearest McDonald's was forty minutes away. Logically, I should go home and eat there, but at that particular moment Nana Cole's house was about as appealing as a nuclear test site.

Also, Opal had left two messages before my phone died. Begrudgingly, I drove out to Queens Way Mobile Home Park in Coldwater. I parked across the street from the park since it was barely plowed. Not that it was easier to park on Turtle Highway, I was just less likely to get stuck—though, more likely to have my car totaled by a semi.

Promising myself I'd be quick, I jumped out of my car and ran across the two narrow lanes of Turtle Highway. Honestly, most places in the country would be embarrassed to call it a highway. I could name wider residential streets in LA, but there you go.

When I knocked on Ronnie Sheck's door, I noticed my hands were getting red and chapped from never wearing gloves. Maybe I needed to pay more attention. No. I reminded myself I wouldn't be here much longer. Worrying about whether I had gloves to wear implied a permanence I couldn't deal with.

Ronnie opened the door, and said, "Oh, you..." He stuck his head out and looked in each direction, didn't see anything, and pulled me inside.

The same two stoned minions who were always there sat zoned out on the rancid looking sofa. Before I could ask another question, he unzipped my puffer coat and stuck his hand up under my sweater.

"Hey, that tickles."

After withdrawing his hand, he said, "Sorry. We've been watching *The Wire* on HBO. It's got me a little freaked out, you know?"

I didn't, so I said, "Whatever."

"I don't have any benzos right now. I do have a big bag of thirties."

Thirties meant Oxy, and despite every bone in my body screaming, "YES! I'LL TAKE THE WHOLE BAG!" I shook my head no.

"You sure? I've got a new source. This guy in Florida, he's got ten or fifteen seniors on payroll. They go from doctor to doctor complaining about arthritis. It's like a freaking faucet."

Apparently, he thought I'd stopped Oxy due to low supply. I said, "Listen, I'm looking for a guy named Denny who works at the barbershop in Masons Bay. He likes to PNP."

"Yeah, so... Why do you care?"

"I don't really. Do you know Opal who works at Pastiche?"

"Dyke."

"Yeah, uh... technically, I think she's bi. Anyway, she's got this thing for Carl Burke, who's also bi, and he has a thing for Denny. And now Denny is missing, which upsets Carl, which upsets Opal, and now it's upsetting me."

"Well, I'm not upset. I don't give a shit where he is."

"He's been gone a couple of days, probably having sex

somewhere. I wondered if you might have some idea where that might be?"

"Yeah, you know, my clients expect a certain amount of confidence, or whatever, so how about you fuck off. If you're not buying, you're leaving."

Okay, well, that was useless. I was about to go when I thought of something. "You showed me that shoebox of random drugs you have. Are there any heart medications in there?"

"I'm not a pharmacist..." he said, then he thought about it, and said, "I mean, amateur, sure, but... Hold on."

Apparently, I'd sparked his curiosity. He walked out of the room, leaving me with his minions who looked like they might chop me up into bits just to break the monotony. Before they could decide about that, Ronnie was back with the shoebox. He picked through it as he walked.

"Crestor? Is that for the heart?"

I had no idea. "Is there anything in there that says Russell Belcher?"

He pushed the bottles around for a moment then said, "Oh yeah. Nitroglycerin?"

One of the minions said, "Boom." He was right. It was the main ingredient in dynamite. But I was pretty sure it was also used to prevent a heart attack. I wasn't sure why I knew that, but...

"Did you get that from Bobbie LaCross?"

"Probably, yeah. I mean she brought in the shoebox, and it was full of meds. Nothing good. I didn't give her much for it. There was an inhaler in there and I sold that for twice what I paid for the box, so it was worth it."

The whole thing was starting to come into focus. Bobbie had stolen the box of medications, presumably to get her hands on the Oxy. Before the drugs could be replaced, Russell had a heart attack and, without his nitroglycerin, died. Patty knew about this and blamed Bobbie, believing she'd killed Russell. Which is why she told me Bobbie had killed a man.

All of that happened about a year ago. The anniversary of Russell's death triggered... Patty to kill Bobbie? No, that didn't make sense. She'd have said why in the confession. The only reason to hide that was... Brian. Brian was the one who'd killed Bobbie. Patty confessed to protect him.

It was a leap, I know, but a good one. I looked closely at Ronnie, and said, "The police will be coming out here sometime soon."

"How do you know that?"

"Patty Gauthier confessed to killing Bobbie, but I don't think she did it. Brian Belcher did. I'm going to go into the sheriff's office and tell them that tomorrow."

Ronnie offered me the shoebox. "Take this and give it to them."

"They're still going to come out here."

"Don't mention my name."

"I think they know your name."

"What the fuck am I supposed to do?"

"When they come out, give them the box. Tell them you collect unused meds and give them to your neighbors—who I'm guessing don't have health insurance. Tell them you traded Bobbie for some high-end allergy meds."

"They're not going to believe that."

"No, they won't. But they won't be able to do anything about it since you'll get everything out of here first."

He thought about it for a long moment, then looked at his minions and motioned for them to start. Turning to me he said, "How about a couple Oxy on the house?"

I couldn't bring myself to say no outright, so I said, "I'll take a raincheck."

Then he said, "Okay. There's a house. It's kind of up behind Masons Bay. On a cul-de-sac. There are like five houses, all snowbirds, sitting empty. People have been partying in there. You might want to check for Denny there."

"Thanks."

When I got out to Turtle Highway my car had not been destroyed by a semi, which was a relief. I climbed in, pulled a U-turn, and headed back at low speed to Masons Bay. I drove directly to Benson's Country Store hoping to buy a sandwich, but unfortunately it was well after seven so they were closed. I sat in their dark empty parking lot thinking about what to do next.

I wanted to call Opal and tell her where Denny might be. She'd have a better idea of where a hillside cul-de-sac of snow-birds might be, but my phone was completely out of juice and wouldn't even come on.

I could just go home and call Opal from the landline while the damn mobile phone charged. But I just wasn't up to running the gauntlet of my grandmother's kitchen. There was a fifty-fifty chance she was furious with me. Well, sixty-forty. Okay, fine, seventy-thirty.

I toyed with the idea of going to Main Street Café and having dinner on my grandmother's credit card but thought about what Ronnie had told me. Behind Masons Bay. Main Street ran parallel to Lake Michigan. There was a marina and a row of condos and a small beach. There was also an arm-shaped peninsula that curled around enough to justify the Bay part of the village's name.

Behind Masons Bay had to mean inland. There were several blocks 'behind' the village slowly rising uphill with the topmost streets having a lake view. The value of houses rose with each view and put the homes out of reach for locals. The cul-de-sac of snowbirds was likely up there.

It wouldn't take too long. I'd just drive around up there and see what I could see. Then I'd either go home and have some dinner while Nana Cole plotted my demise, or I'd go ahead and pop into Main Street Café and have a burger.

I'd been up that way before. I'd gone to a book club meeting on Meadowlark Lane—and gotten stabbed—just a few months ago. I didn't recall any cul-de-sacs, but then I wasn't looking for one. I drove back and forth on Meadowlark Lane until I noticed a road that went further up the hill—I missed it the first time I passed.

The streets behind Masons Bay did have streetlights but not many, and the road that went further up the hill had none. Nor a street sign. I turned onto it and drove upward. Slowly—my car didn't do hills well. Or snow. Or snowy hills.

I came across a street on the right and turned into it, and found myself in a cul-de-sac. Well that was easy, I thought, before I realized that two of the houses had well-plowed drive-ways and all their lights were on. People were at home. In the winter. This was not what Ronnie had described.

I turned around in a circle and went back to the road I'd come up. I turned right and continued up the hill. The next road I came to was on my left. I turned onto that road, only to find that it wasn't a cul-de-sac. Or at least it didn't seem like one at first. It was a straight road, four houses on each side of the road, none of which seemed occupied. Two of them were still for sale with signs from The Hanson Group.

At the end of the street I was going to turn around, but I noticed another road. This one was poorly plowed but had several rows of tire tracks through the snow. I decided it was probably wise to not try driving my car up that way. I parked and turned out the lights. It got very dark. Getting out, I zipped up my puffer coat, pulled the hat down tighter onto my head, and crammed the keys into my pocket.

Then I went around to the trunk. Shortly after my mother abandoned us and the snow began to fly, my grandmother told me I couldn't bring the baby in my car unless I got an emergency kit for my trunk. So now I drove around with a couple of road flares, reflectors, a tiny tool kit, tweezers, a flashlight, a plastic poncho, jumper cables, a tow rope, a first aid kit, gloves and a folding shovel. Half of it seemed useless in an emergency, but there you go. I found the flashlight, useful in this non-emergency, and walked up the hill.

Yes, this was another cul-de-sac. One that seemed particularly unoccupied. The houses were dark, the driveways unplowed, and there was only one vehicle to be seen. A red Thunderbird from the late eighties. Denny's Thunderbird. I'd seen him in it. He was very likely in one of the four houses on the cul-de-sac. They were all dark though.

I walked over to the Thunderbird. It had been there a day or two since there was three inches of snow on it. I pointed the flashlight through the windows to confirm the car was empty. It was. With my flashlight, I began looking through the snow for footprints. It made sense to start with the two houses closest to Denny's car.

I found dimpled footsteps going up the driveway of the furthest house. It was a recent, two-story house with a giant garage. I followed the footprints around to the side of the garage where they disappeared in front of a door. It was standing open, taking the unlocked door thing to a whole new level.

Stepping into the garage, I found that these snowbirds left a Jeep with a canvas top for summer use. Hanging from the open ceiling was a canoe, against the back wall were four bicycles leaning on one another. The door from the garage to the house stood open, which couldn't be good for their heating bill.

Yes, they weren't here, but you still had to heat the place—I'd learned this from random conversations. Generally, people left their thermostats at fifty when they left for the winter. It saved them money and prevented the pipes from bursting.

The door led directly into the kitchen. I went ahead and turned a light on. I mean, the entire neighborhood was vacated. Yeah, someone might notice the light through the trees, but I doubted they'd call the sheriff even if they did notice it.

The kitchen was a mess: a pizza box, a case worth of empty beer cans, several full ashtrays, a couple of vodka bottles—one of which was half full, a pile of rust-stained paper towels. That was blood. Not a lot. Not a murder amount of blood—I'd seen that before. This was more like nosebleed blood.

It was warm, very warm. Someone had turned the heat up and that wasn't making the smell any better: cigarette smoke mixed with marijuana smoke, a sewer kind of smell that suggested I was going to find a stopped-up toilet, and something sour I couldn't quite place.

The living room was in much the same condition as the kitchen: large coffee table held a bong, more beer cans, glasses, plates used as ashtrays, bits of aluminum foil, pipes, razor blades, rolled up dollar bills. Two expensive sofas sat on either side of the coffee table facing each other. Their seat cushions were on the floor. I could see that there were cigarette burns in both. This was going to be an insurance claim.

I went up the stairs, turning lights on as I went. I went into the first bedroom I came to and there was Denny. He was lying naked on a stripped bed. He had a look of surprise on his pale, waxy face. It didn't take a medical degree to figure out he was dead. I was standing in the middle of a crime scene.

I really need to stop doing that.

CHAPTER NINETEEN

After I used the house phone to call 9-1-1, I went out and sat in my car. He'd obviously died of an overdose of some kind. Tweaked himself to death. Honestly, it should have been more upsetting. And it might have been if I hadn't popped three Ativan right before I made the call. Three was my limit. Four and I would sleep for eight or nine hours. Three would make me drowsy, but the adrenaline produced by finding a dead body would counteract that. Yup, three was exactly right.

I should have called Opal while I was still in the house. Not that I'd memorized her number—and not that I could turn my cell phone back on. So even if I'd thought about it, I couldn't have. I really needed one of those phone chargers you plugged into a car's cigarette lighter. And I'd probably have one if I hadn't been so busy lately. Although, I always seemed to be... Whatever.

Deputy Twiss showed up, which was annoying. It was late, you'd think he'd have gone home. He'd probably been napping at the sheriff's office while making triple overtime. He certainly looked like I'd woken him up.

"I got a call about a dead body?"

"Yeah, in that house there. Second floor, first bedroom. Guy named Denny. Drug overdose."

Before I finished, I realized I should have called this in anonymously. It was going to be hard to explain.

"Whose house is it?"

"I don't know."

"What were you doing in there?"

"I was looking for Denny."

"Denny... What?"

"I don't know his last name." I'd forgotten it. Three Ativan, remember?

"You broke into a random house, looking for a guy whose name you don't know. Am I getting this right?"

"I didn't break into the house. The doors were open."

"You were trespassing, then."

I was probably trespassing but... "That's Denny's car. The Thunderbird. He works at his dad's barbershop."

"Denny Hazzard."

Crap, I should have remembered that. He was aptly named.

"Sure. Denny Hazzard is on the second floor. Don't you want to go in and see?"

"Why were you looking for him?"

"A friend asked me to."

"Why did you look for him here?"

"I heard that people do meth in these summer houses sometimes."

"You heard from who?"

"The grapevine."

"You're sure he died of a drug overdose?"

"No. I'm not the coroner."

Another of the sheriff's SUVs pulled up and a deputy got out. Twiss nodded toward the house.

"Is Detective Lehmann on his way?" I asked.

"You said drug overdose. Do you think Denny was murdered?"

"There's no blood, so he wasn't stabbed or shot. It didn't look like he was strangled or anything. Plus, he was a drug addict."

"So, we don't need Lehmann, do we?"

"Can I go then?"

"I'm still thinking about charging you with trespass."

"Then I should call my lawyer."

He chewed on that for a moment, then said, "You can go. I know where you live."

THEY WERE LAUGHING and playing pinocle when I got home. Emerald was sitting upright in a playpen from the sixties that had been set up on the floor. I'd specifically said no to playpens after a conversation with a woman in the formula aisle at the Meijer over in Traverse.

So much information in those first few seconds, I was having trouble sorting it out.

"There you are," Barbara said. "We brought a pizza from The Wagon Wheel; we saved you a few pieces. I'll heat it up."

She got up while I hung up my puffer jacket and kicked my boots off.

"Play my hand for me," Barbara said.

"I don't know how to play."

"Neither does she," Nana Cole said, and then cackled. That's when I realized there were wine glasses on the table. She was drunk.

"Emerald is sitting up all by herself," I said—mostly to avoid saying all the things I shouldn't, like they're talking, they're drinking, the baby's in a playpen even though—

"Oh, she's been doing that for days. You've been running around so much you missed it. It's your play."

There were two cards sitting in the middle of the table. I picked up Barbara's hand, five cards, and said, "I have no idea what to play."

Bev looked at my hand, and said, "Play the king of hearts."

I actually had two kings of hearts, which seemed wrong, but then I didn't know the rules. I played the king, and Bev said, "There, you won the trick."

"With your help," Nana Cole said.

"He doesn't know what he's doing."

"He never does."

"Hey."

Barbara interrupted with, "Henry, would you like a glass of wine?"

Given the Ativan in my system, I'd likely fall right to sleep. I said, "Absolutely."

"It's your lead," Nana Cole said.

"My what?"

"You play first."

"Play the ace of trump," Barbara said, as she poured my glass of wine.

"What's trump?"

"Barbara, he can get his own pizza, sit back down and play."

I gave Barbara her seat. I leaned against the counter next to the stove making faces at my sister and sipping wine.

"Where've you been all night?" Nana Cole asked.

I was sure she thought I'd staged the whole thing to get them all talking again and had probably just gone to a movie, so I was pleased to say, "Oh, yeah, Brian Belcher is the one who really killed Bobbie LaCross. I'm going to go and explain that to Detective Lehmann in the morning. And Denny Hazzard died of an overdose. I found his body."

That stopped the card game. The women just stared at me for a moment. Finally, Nana Cole said, "And you're just sitting here playing cards and not saying a word?"

Apparently, she'd forgotten the part where she made me sit down and play a game I didn't know the rules to.

"Poor Joe," Barbara said.

"It's been coming," Bev said.

And that made me wonder if anyone in this place knew what a secret was. Obviously, no one kept them.

"Was it murder?" Nana Cole asked. "Did someone kill Joe's boy?"

"No. I don't think so."

"Well, what do you know?"

"You just asked me. Why ask me if you're not going to believe what I say?"

"If you found him, you must have seen something. Bruising, scratches, blood, bullet holes."

"Nana, there was none of that. I really think he overdosed." And then, to change the subject, I asked, "Are you going to ask how I figured out it was Brian Belcher who killed Bobbie?"

They stared at me a moment until Barbara said, "Well, tell us."

After I caught them up, I got the pizza out of the oven and took a bite. It wasn't bad, but the Ativan had killed my hunger. I just nibbled.

"I don't believe it," Nana Cole said. "Brian Belcher is so much younger than Patty. They can't possibly be involved."

"I don't know," Bev said. "Patty is still an attractive woman." A sentence that now sounded much different than it would have just days before.

"I think it's romantic," Barbara said. "Confessing like that to save the man you love."

"Stupid is more like it," Nana Cole said. "She'll go to prison, and he'll find some young tramp and that'll be that."

"Well, that won't happen," Barbara said. "Henry's going to tell the sheriff what's really happening. And then it will all work out."

Even I thought that was unlikely, but I nodded agreement anyway. A few minutes later, Bev and Barbara said it was time to go. Once they got their coats and gloves and hats on, Barbara asked, "Do you need me to come back in the morning so you can go to the sheriff?"

"It's okay. I'll just bring Emerald along. I think Detective Lehmann likes her."

"You can leave her with me," Nana Cole said, grumpily. "I'm not completely helpless."

"I'll bring her with me."

After they walked out the door, I picked up the baby and said, "We're going to go upstairs and go to bed." I should probably have left it at that, but I had to say, "I'm glad things are better."

She shrugged and said, "Nobody cares what a couple of old ladies do."

Okay, that was a challenge. Did she mean their gayness would matter if they were younger? Did she mean it would matter if they were a couple of old men? And she, an old lady herself, couldn't really believe it didn't matter what old ladies did—could she?

Showing incredible restraint, I said, "Okay then," and we went upstairs to bed.

CHAPTER TWENTY

Emerald slept for six hours without waking up, so I did too. That was amazing. We were up around five. I was a little groggy, so I barely remember changing her, tickling her until she was giggling, and then bringing her downstairs for a breakfast of rice cereal and crushed blueberries.

I do remember that the baby—and I—were covered with mushy blueberries when the landline rang. I grabbed it before the second ring, getting blueberries and cereal all over the receiver. The phone, the high chair, the baby and I were now covered. Had I gotten any breakfast into Emerald?

"Hello," I whispered into the phone. The last thing I wanted to do was wake up my grandmother.

"How could you not call me!" Opal screamed.

And that was when I realized I'd never plugged my phone into the charger. It was sitting on my desk upstairs still dead.

"Um, my phone died."

"Your phone died! Your phone died? Denny died!"

"I know. I'm the one who found him."

"Carl found out on MySpace."

I'd heard of MySpace. I should sign up. It sounds like it might be useful.

"I'm sorry. But you know, it sucks no matter how Carl found out."

"He's devastated."

"I'm sure he is."

"I'm going over to his house. You should come with me."

"No. I really shouldn't."

"He's going to have questions."

"He doesn't want the answers I have."

"Okay... so lie."

"No problem. 'I heard that people had broken into this summer house to... do light drugs and have intellectual conversations. Denny was so interested in the conversations he stayed there for days and did lots and lots of the light, almost harmless drugs that his heart exploded, which couldn't possibly have been as painful as it sounds because he died with a look of satisfied contentment on his face.' Is that what you want me to say?"

"Somewhere in between that and what you actually saw. I'll pick you up in forty-five minutes."

I hung up the blueberry-coated phone. I planned to go outside and tell her no again when she arrived, which didn't mean I had nothing to do. First, I needed to wipe down my sister. Then I'd put her into the playpen long enough to take a shower.

Playpens were much more useful than I thought, and I probably should have relented and brought it out before now. I really should pay less attention to random women I meet at Meijer than I had been. I mean, ten minutes in a playpen was unlikely to scar my sister for life. And if it did leave a scar, it was unlikely to be worse than the scars growing up with my mother would leave.

I knew my mother would come back at some point. Hopefully before Emerald was potty-trained, though after was a distinct possibility. Maybe she and her new husband would be heading back to Los Angeles and I could hitch a ride. With her and the baby. She might even need a sitter.

Having a new stepfather was always a problem. This one was rich, of course. Usually they had some money, but this one really seemed to have a lot. Enough to go bankrupt. Or rather, his company was going bankrupt. Bankruptcy for rich people was like plastic surgery, painful while it was happening but rejuvenating afterward. My guess was David would be rich again by the time my mother reappeared.

It was barely six o'clock in the morning when Opal showed up. My grandmother wasn't awake yet. The *Today* show hadn't even started. I had dressed Emerald in the pink snowsuit my mother had sent. It was labeled nine months, but it fit her just fine. I got her tucked into her car seat and she began to fuss. So I gave her the plastic keys, which I knew would buy me a few minutes.

I put on my puffer coat, my Bassett Hound hat and stepped into my boots. Of course, I wasn't going with Opal. I'd explain that when she got there then maybe go out to breakfast —though I couldn't think of anyplace open before seven. Then after breakfast, I'd go to the sheriff's office to talk with Detective Lehmann.

That was the plan, but then Opal was in the driveway honking her horn. That had to stop, she was going to wake up my grandmother and that wouldn't be good. I grabbed the car seat and hurried out the back door. I went directly to the driver's side.

She rolled down the window, and said, "Get in."

"I'm not going with you."

"You look like you're going with me."

"I'm taking myself out for breakfast."

"Where? No place is open until seven."

I didn't have a good answer to that. Obviously, I wasn't going to sit out in front of a restaurant in the middle of winter with a baby in the car. So, what *would* I do?

"I can't stay very long. I have to go to the sheriff's office."

"Get in."

I might not have, but I noticed my grandmother had gotten up and was now looking out at us through the porch window. I wrangled the baby seat into the back of the ladybug—which, by the way, is challenging enough to suggest it might merit its own Olympic event—and then climbed into the passenger seat.

As she pulled out onto M-22, Opal said, "The visual of you with a baby is really wrong."

"Thank you. I assume that's a compliment."

"It's not."

We were silent until we were driving through the village of Masons Bay. As we passed Pastiche, she asked, "How did you find him?"

"I went to see Ronnie, like you asked me to. He said he'd heard about the house they were using."

"Do you think Ronnie sold it to him? The meth that killed him?"

The was an emphatic yes. Probably. But what I said was, "I don't know. Does it matter?"

"And you have no idea who he might have been with?"

"No idea."

I could tell she wanted someone to blame. Someone other than Denny. But this wasn't like other situations where someone sold you something and it killed you—it wasn't a car that exploded on impact and you had assumed it was safe. It wasn't a new drug that had a nasty side effect of giving people strokes. No, this was a situation where Denny knew exactly what might happen. He knew that meth might kill him. And he had to have known the longer he took it the more likely it was that it *would* kill him. None of this was a surprise.

"It's Denny's own fault."

"Don't say that to Carl. If he wants to blame the man in the moon let him."

"The man in the moon isn't real."

"And stop taking things literally. At least for an hour."

Carl Burke lived with his mother, Ivy Greene, north of Masons Bay a half a mile from Patty Gauthier. M-22 turned inland around there and began to climb, which was why Ivy Greene's lot was much larger than Patty's. Patty's house took up nearly her entire lot, while Ivy's was built into the side of a hill and sloped down to the water.

The house was surrounded by trees, mostly evergreen and, given all the snow, looked like it belonged in the Alps. It was three stories, an odd three stories. The front door led into what was really the cellar. You went through the laundry room into a family room. I assumed there was a living room upstairs with a kitchen, dining room and bedrooms, though I'd never been there.

We knocked and waited. When nothing happened, Opal pushed the unlocked door open and went in.

"Really?"

"We have a baby with us. We can't stay out here in the cold." Then she called out, "Ivy! Carl!"

From deep in the house, Ivy called out, "Coming."

We went into the family room with its beat-up leather sectional and TV. Emerald was beginning to fuss, so I unbelted her and took her out of the car seat. I bounced her around and swung her back and forth until she was giggling. Opal stared at us, and then muttered, "So wrong."

Ivy came down the stairs. She was in her mid-forties but looked much younger, had dyed red hair which needed a touch up, and her lips were beginning to crease from having been pursed so much. Immediately, she walked over to Opal and hugged her.

"Thank you for coming. Carl needs his friends." Then she looked at me with a touch of confusion. "I didn't know you and Carl were close. Or do you just show up when people die?"

"Henry's the one who found Denny. I thought he might be able to answer any questions Carl had."

She looked at me suspiciously, as though I might suddenly start attacking people, but then Emerald let out a burp much too large for someone her size.

"My goodness. Is this your sister?"

"Emerald."

"May I?" Ivy held her arms out to take the baby. I passed her over.

It's strange the way we pass babies around. They're precious things, valuable. We'd never dream of asking to hold other valuable things. If I had a rare piece of ancient pottery, no one would say, 'oh lemme hold it' and if they did, and I said, 'no' they'd understand. But if I said, 'No, you can't hold my sister, she's too precious' no one would understand. Reluctantly, I handed her over.

After making a bunch of ridiculous sounds at my sister, Ivy asked me, "And how is your mother?"

"I wouldn't know."

"That's right. I heard that she abandoned her baby. Although, I don't know how she could. Emmie's just so adorable."

"Emerald," I corrected.

Here's the thing about relatives. When I say my mother abandoned us—and yes, I know I say that a lot—it's one thing. But when other people say it, well, it's vaguely insulting.

"She had some things to take care of," I said, holding my arms out for me sister.

Reluctantly, Ivy gave the baby back to me. Then asked, "What sort of things?"

"She got married to Emerald's father."

"Oh, that's lovely. How was the wedding?"

"Small."

"You probably want to take her out of that snowsuit while she's inside. You don't want her to overheat."

"We won't be here long."

Opal stomped on my foot. I gritted my teeth as I waited for the pain to subside.

There was a noise on the stairs and Carl came down. Ivy hurried over to the bottom of the stairs, nearly knocking Opal over. "Sweetheart, if it's too much you don't have to come down."

"I want to see Opal."

"All right. She's right here."

Carl had reached the bottom of the stairs. He looked smaller somehow. He was still tall, thin, and sharply drawn, but now... well it was like the difference between a watercolor and ink sketch. Denny's death had drawn the color from him and left only dark scratches.

"Well," Ivy said. "I've got coffee upstairs and cinnamon buns. I'll bring them down."

"You didn't need to come," Carl said as his mother went upstairs.

"Yes, I did. I'm so sorry, Carl," Opal said.

"I meant him."

Great. I didn't want to be there and he didn't want me there. This was going to be pleasant.

"He found Denny. I knew you'd have questions."

His eyes flared, and he demanded, "Who killed him? Who killed Denny?"

"It was an overdose."

"Were you there?"

"No. Of course not. I don't do... meth." Nor would I lower my standards enough to find people to have sex with while on—

"Then how do you know he wasn't murdered?"

He had me there. I wasn't one hundred percent certain, but Denny was known to be an addict, was found in a location where people were known to be doing drugs, he was naked, and there didn't seem to be any indication of another cause of death.

"The sheriff didn't send Detective Lehmann. They don't consider it a suspicious death."

"The sheriff is an idiot. And he lives in Florida."

"Well, there's that," I had to admit. "But, honestly..." And here a lie seemed appropriate. "He looked peaceful. I'm not sure people who are murdered look peaceful."

Yes, he looked more surprised than peaceful. But surprised didn't mean murdered either. Murdered would be terror, horror, anger... and mostly fear. There had been fear on Bobbie's face and there had been none of that on Denny's.

Ivy came down the stairs with a tray holding a pot of coffee, mugs, cream and sugar, and the cinnamon rolls. She put the tray down on the coffee table, and said, "Help yourselves."

I put Emerald back in the car seat and sat down across from the coffee, poured myself a cup and put a roll on a napkin. I was starving. And if I'm being honest, still a bit groggy from the Ativan I'd had the night before.

"He was murdered," Carl said to his mother.

I had a mouthful of cinnamon roll, so all I could do was shake my head and mumble, "I middn't zay..."

"Let's wait to see what the sheriff says," Ivy said.

"They don't care. You know they don't care."

"Henry's working for a private investigator," Opal said.

"Really?" Ivy said. "How odd."

"He could look into it. And he wouldn't charge you."

"Excuse me?" I'd managed to swallow. I also managed to move my foot before Opal could stomp on it.

"Would you?" Carl asked. "Would you do that?"

I really wanted to say no. I mean, it was obviously an overdose. One that Carl should have seen coming a long time ago. On the other hand, I realized it would get me out of there if I played it...

"I could talk to Detective Lehmann for you. See if there's any reason to suspect it wasn't an overdose. In fact, I'm due at the sheriff's office soon. Opal's going to drive me there."

"At seven-thirty in the morning?" Ivy asked.

"They're open twenty-four seven."

CHAPTER TWENTY-ONE

"I'll pay you if I really have to," Opal said as we pulled out onto M-22 on our way to the Municipal Center.

Even though she always had one or two crappy jobs, she apparently had a lot of money. That made me doubt her sanity, since if I had a lot of money I'd be gone from Wyandot County in a heartbeat.

"There isn't anything to investigate."

"You told them you'd talk to Detective Lehmann about it."

"And I will, but I know he's going to tell me Denny overdosed."

"And you're going to ask why he thinks that."

If that was her idea of investigating, then I'd do it. There was an irony here that wasn't lost on me. Usually, or at least in the last year, it was me saying "this isn't what it looks like". And then I'd prove it wasn't what it looked like. But now, with Denny, I was saying this is exactly what it looks like, and no one wanted to believe me.

The sun was finally coming up when we parked in front of the sheriff's office. It promised to be another gray, snowy day. I got Emerald out of the backseat.

My first indication that something was happening was

Bernie's Jetta sitting in the parking lot. There was also a black Mercedes from the early nineties, the weird Subaru and half a dozen other cars.

I made Opal stop in the lobby so I could open up Emerald's snowsuit and roll it down. She'd fallen asleep on the way over and now she let out a wail at being woken. Once I was sure she wasn't going to roast to death, I swung the car seat back and forth until she calmed down. Then we went into the sheriff's office.

In the common area, there was a lot going on for seven-thirty in the morning. Deputy Twiss was already there—dreaming of his overtime check, I'm sure. Bernie was sitting pensively looking at Patty Gauthier, and I could hear yelling—or at least strong, forceful statements, coming out of the inter-view room.

I tried to set Emerald on a desk, but the lack of movement made her grumble, the grumble before the wail. I took her off the desk and swung the car seat back and forth.

I asked Bernie, "What's going on?"

"Brian Belcher is in there confessing to Bobbie's murder."

"He didn't do it," Patty insisted. "It was me."

Ignoring her—I assumed it wasn't the first time that morning she'd ignored his advice and made that inadvisable statement—Bernie asked me, "What are you doing here?"

"I came to tell Detective Lehmann that Brian's the one who killed Bobbie."

"But he didn't. It was me," Patty said. "And I'm not paying you to accuse my... friend."

"Okay, but isn't it my job to get you out of trouble?"

"No. It is not."

I looked at Bernie, and said, "Can we step over here and chat?"

"Yeah, sure."

I offered Opal the car seat, and asked, "Could you?"

"Are you insane? My maternal instinct died with Punky Brewster."

Punky Brewster was not dead, but I got her point.

"I'll take her," Patty said.

I was a horrible brother, handing my sister over to a confessed murderer.

"Just rock the car seat—"

She'd already put the car seat on a desk and was releasing Emerald from its clutches.

"Or... that."

Bernie pulled me into an empty office and shut the door. I peeked through a window that was located next to the door, and watched Patty bounce my sister and coo at her. Opal watched them in disgust.

"So... what do you have?"

"Patty and Brian are romantically involved."

"Yeah, I figured that out."

"Brian's father died last year of a heart attack. They blame Bobbie because she stole a shoebox full of his medicines, including his heart meds."

"You think that's what he's telling Lehmann?"

"Yes."

"Any evidence they did it together?"

I hadn't thought of that. What would it be, though? Phone messages, texts, notes, diagrams, overheard conversations. None of which I had.

"Why would each confess if they did it together?"

"Because his defense is that she confessed and her defense is that he confessed. Reasonable doubt. Lehmann is going to need something more. A witness, or something forensic."

"Do you want me to—"

"No, no, no... nada. Don't do anything else. We want to cross our fingers and hope Lehmann can't find anything."

"You don't want me to do anything, really?" That didn't feel right.

"Not a thing."

Then we heard a commotion. Bernie opened the door, and we went back out. Detective Lehmann was standing there with Brian Belcher and an older man I didn't recognize. He had gray hair, and a scowl that made anger look like a genetic condition.

Patty was crying, still holding my sister.

"Brian, Brian you shouldn't—" To Lehmann she said, "He's just trying to save me. Don't you see that?"

I rushed over and took Emerald back. My sister had a confused look on her face. She wasn't used to other people crying. She was also very moist and in need of a change.

"I hope you understand, if you dare charge my client I'll make sure you regret it every day for the rest of your life," anger-man said. It surprised me that he'd waited until they opened the door to threaten Detective Lehmann.

Though, glancing at the detective's face suggested there many have been quite a few threats issued during the interview.

"Come along, Brian."

As they began to leave, anger-man gave Bernie a nasty look and then stopped in front of me saying, "You're Henry Milch."

"Yeah." I did not want to talk to this guy.

He looked me up and down. Seriously, not an expression. He looked at my feet and then took in every inch of me all the way up to the top of my head. Then he said, "Jesus Christ," and walked away.

After a moment, I asked, "What was that?"

"My father. Bernard Schaub," Bernie said.

"You have my deepest sympathy."

Without acknowledging me, Bernie shifted gears and said, "Rudy, you need to release my client immediately. You've had another confession. If you're not holding him, you can't hold her."

Lehmann rolled his eyes, and said, "Gimme five minutes. I need to do some paperwork."

Once he was gone, Patty asked, "Is that it? Is it over?"

"Not exactly," Bernie said. "You're going to need to watch your step. Lehmann is going to be going through your phone records, your bank records, everything he can think of looking for some kind of evidence that the two of you conspired to kill Bobbie LaCross."

"He won't find it. It was just me."

There was the tiniest pause and then Opal rushed in with, "Dude, you really need to change that baby's diaper."

I hurried off to the restroom. Honestly, the introduction of actual food to Emerald's diet had not helped things in the diaper department. While I was trying not to think about what I was seeing—and smelling—I wondered what was really going on here. Had Patty and Brian colluded to avenge his father's death? Was it right for them to get away with it?

Certainly, what Bobbie did was terrible, but she hadn't meant for it to result in Russell Belcher's death. Then I wondered if that was negligent homicide or involuntary manslaughter. Should Brian have simply turned her in? Would that have worked? They probably couldn't prove Bobbie took the box of meds. I mean, I could prove it now—her fingerprints were probably on the shoebox. And even if they'd been able to prove it, would it have stood up?

I wondered what motive Brian had given in his confession. Had he explained about the drugs to Detective Lehmann? Would being able to prove that help or hurt the case against him? It might make a jury sympathetic. It made me sympathetic. You never stole *all* of someone's meds. That was not a good idea.

I finished up the diaper change, washed my hands, and went back into the sheriff's office. Detective Lehmann was standing with Bernie and Patty. Opal sat at a desk ten feet away. I walked over as Bernie was saying, "So you've no evidence aside from my client's coerced confession?"

"Not coerced—"

"I assume you had forensics go over the RV Ms. LaCross was living in. Did you find my clients fingerprints?"

"No."

"Did you find anyone's fingerprints other than the deceased?"

"We haven't identified all the fingerprints we found."

"Which one's have you identified?"

"Well, only Buford Campbell. But he owns the RV, so it's not unusual to find those."

Bernie considered the detective for a moment, then said,

"Thank you, Rudy. Should you have any questions for my client please don't contact her directly. Contact me and we'll set up a time to meet."

Lehmann grinned like a pit bull baring its teeth. Then, spinning on a heel, he turned and went into his office. I followed him in, stopping the door before it shut, then closing it behind me. Emerald was pulling on my hair, which hurt, but I ignored it.

From behind his desk, Lehmann said, "I'm going to need a statement from you."

"About?" I gently untangled my sister's fist from my hair, and she immediately grabbed another clump.

"You found a dead body last night. Or has that slipped your mind?"

"No, I'm here to talk to you about that. Do you know when you'll have the autopsy report?" I tried holding my sister lower, so she couldn't reach my hair. Now she pulled on my sweater, instead.

"The postmortem we'll have in about a week. The toxicology report should take a month or so. Why?"

"His friends think it might be murder."

He raised an eyebrow. "Why?"

"I guess it's easier than thinking he did it to himself."

A random thought: If I'd died when I overdosed would anyone have thought it was murder, would they have hoped it was murder, so they didn't have to think about me doing it to myself? Of course, I did make a mistake once. Did Denny make a mistake, or was this what he was planning all along?

"You don't think it was murder, do you?" I asked.

Looking tired, he sat down and said, "There'd have to be something very weird in the autopsy. But right now? No."

"Did Brian talk to you about the box of medications Bobbie stole from his father?"

His face told me he had, even as he said, "I can't talk to you about that."

"If you want the box, Ronnie Scheck has it."

"That's interesting."

"Don't get too excited. He knows you're coming. I doubt there will even be an aspirin in that trailer by the time you get there." I was about to leave, partly because my sister was squirming so much I thought I might drop her, when I wondered about something.

"Everybody knows what Ronnie's up to, how come he never gets arrested?"

Lehmann shrugged, then said, "The devil you know... that's how it was explained to me."

CHAPTER TWENTY-TWO

"Did the detective say what we should expect from the autopsy?" Opal asked as we passed through Masons Bay Village.

He had not, but I decided to answer anyway, relying on my extensive viewing of *CSI: Wherever*. "The autopsy will probably show evidence of a heart attack. And the toxicology report will show that he was taking methamphetamine, which brought on the heart attack."

She frowned. "And if it was murder, what will it show?"

"There was no blood, so he wasn't shot or stabbed. I suppose he could have been strangled. The autopsy might show that his throat was compressed, or his hy-hy-something bone was broken. If he was poisoned by something other than meth it will be in the toxicology report."

We drove for a bit and she didn't say anything.

"You knew where this was heading, it's why you wanted me to find him."

"Carl wanted to save him."

"An addict can only save themselves."

Guess who's been paying attention at meetings? Me! Not that I really believe any of it. I'm sure there were lots of reasons to quit drugs that weren't me. For example, I quit Oxy so I could take care of my sister.

I didn't save myself; she saved me.

We turned into my grandmother's driveway, and up by the house sat a recent model Honda Civic, silver, with a USC sticker on the back. I had no idea who that was. The only person I knew in the area who'd gone to USC was Edward, and there was no reason for him to show up—and also no reason for him to drive a Honda Civic. Seriously, why waste all that time becoming a doctor if you had to drive a Civic?

Before getting out, I waited a moment for some kind of thank-you. It didn't come, so I said, "Bye," and opened the door.

"Don't forget the baby."

"I wasn't going to."

"I flipped the seat forward, awkwardly leaned into the backseat, and undid the car seat. Emerald began to fuss. Pulling the car seat and the diaper bag out of the car, I nearly fell over. Opal was watching with a big smile. I slammed the door, which made my sister scream.

She was still screaming when we walked into the kitchen. At the table with Nana Cole was Edward. He wore green scrubs and a pair of leather clogs with blood on them. I got the feeling he'd come in a hurry, as soon as his shift ended.

"The doctor's making a house call," Nana Cole said.

I didn't believe that for a minute. Something else was going on. Something he didn't want to tell my grandmother.

"Emma's recovering nicely from her fall." Then he stood up, "Well, I should be going."

I needed to figure out what was happening. Also, I didn't mind getting away from a screaming baby for a moment, so I said, "I'll walk you to your car." To Nana Cole, I said, "I'll only be a minute. I'll take Emerald out of the car seat when I get back inside. *Leave her in it.*"

She gave me a dirty look as I set the car seat on the table

and the diaper bag on the floor. Then I walked out the back door. Edward was only a few feet behind me. When we got to the Civic, I asked, "Why are you here?"

"It's stupid. I was in the cafeteria earlier and I overheard some nurses talking. I heard the words 'overdose' and then your name and since you hadn't come through the ER, I thought..."

"You thought I was dead?"

"I drove over hoping I was wrong."

"It was Denny Hazzard. He overdosed. I found his body. It was nice of you to worry, though."

"You know, overdosing isn't the only bad thing that can happen to you when you take opioids."

"Yes, I've heard that."

"Brain damage, liver damage, kidney damage, depression, altered personality, low testosterone, osteoporosis..."

"Okay, okay. I get it."

He really should have listed conversations like this one as a side effect. Then something hit me... He said osteoporosis. Was that why...

"Bobbie LaCross broke two bones in the last few years. That was because she was an addict, wasn't it?"

"She was occasionally a patient, so... hypothetically, yes. And, hypothetically, it was three bones."

"Three? She broke her arm, her wrist.... And?"

"Fibula," he said reluctantly.

"What is that?"

"You have two bones in your lower leg. One in the front and another in the back. It helps keep you stable."

"How might a person break that?"

"Slipping in the shower."

"And when might a person have done that?"

"A month ago."

"Really? No. I saw her body. There was no cast."

"Casts aren't used much anymore. They cause muscle

atrophy and extend healing time. A fibula fracture requires an orthopedic boot. It can be taken off to shower and to sleep."

"It was her left leg, wasn't it?"

"It was. How did you figure that out?"

"She was still driving."

What did this mean? Did it mean something? She fell in the shower a month ago. So she'd have been living in the RV on the Campbell compound. Buford seemed annoyed by her being there. Was he annoyed enough to kill her? He said he saw Melanie bring her home, making her a suspect. Did he realize that and then go over and...

"Um, excuse me," Edward said.

"Oh, sorry."

"I have to go now. I just want to say... I'm really glad you're alive. And I'd really like it if you'd stay that way."

"Yeah, me too."

He started to walk away from me, then turned around and said, "Okay... yes."

"Yes, what?"

"We could go out... again. As long as you're not..."

"I'm not. Honest."

"Okay then. I'll give you a call. I find out my schedule in a couple of days."

I stood in the driveway and watched him leave. As I waved, I kept thinking *God, he's so gorgeous. And he cares whether I'm alive or dead.* Actually, I shouldn't put too much stock in the that. It's sort of baseline for a doctor.

God, he's so gorgeous. And we're going out on a date. Soon. And then he was out on M-22 driving away.

When I walked back into the kitchen, I was confronted with the image of my grandmother with her finger in Emerald's mouth and a bottle of whiskey sitting on the table. I took off my boots, and asked, "What do you think you're doing?"

"She's teething. It helps with the pain."

"It's whiskey."

"It's medicinal."

I took Emerald out of the car seat, which was probably the actual problem, and bounced her around until I got her smiling.

"See, it's working," Nana Cole said.

I just her gave a doubtful look and took Emerald upstairs. I put my phone on the charger, finally, and then took the baby into her room and got her out of the snow suit. She'd be growing out of it in a few weeks, which was fine because it really was a pretty pointless garment. We'd basically spent the morning going from a warm car to warm rooms. You really only needed a snow suit if you were planning to take your baby hunting or ice skating or on an expedition to the north pole. And since I was planning none of those, I'd probably never put it on her again. She'd been sweating most of the time and was going to need a bath later.

In the meantime, I put her in a nice clean onesie. Then brought her into my room, got onto the bed, and opened one of the books I'd bought her. *The Very Hungry Caterpillar*. The nice thing about reading to a baby Emerald's age is that you don't have to pay a lot of attention. Particular when her main interest in the book seemed to be chewing on it. Maybe she *was* teething.

Was it possible that Patty Gauthier confessed because she thought Brian Belcher did it? And then Brian confessed, not because he'd done it, but he thought Patty did it and wanted to get her out of trouble? Was it possible that neither of them had done it?

When I felt like I'd waited long enough, I took my phone off the charger and called Ham.

"Hwooo?"

I'd woken him up. What time was it? Crap, it was ten before nine and I'd already had a long day. I was nearly ready for a nap.

"I woke you up. I'm sorry, do you want me to call you back."

"No, no... it's okay. I was up late on a case. What's going on?"

I caught him up on that morning's events, and he said, "I'll call Bernie. Sounds like we're done. I just need to confirm it."

"Actually..."

"I don't like the sound of that."

"You said Bobbie was litigious, right? Is there a way to find out if she was suing anyone else?"

"Uh... you didn't read the whole file I sent you, did you?"

Oh crap.

"It was a lot of paper."

"What brought this about?"

"I found out Bobbie fell in the shower of the RV she was living in. Broke her fibula. It occurred to me she might be suing over it."

"Yeah, I don't think so. The suit against Three Friends is the only one that concerns a broken bone."

"Right. Okay, well, I guess it's nothing then."

"Read the rest of the file."

And then he hung up. I reached over onto my desk, grabbed the Three Friends file, settled in on the bed with my sister tucked onto my lap, and I began to read to her: "Once upon a time there was a horrible old lady who liked to sue people..."

Look, it's not like she's going to remember.

"State of Michigan, Wyandot County Municipal Court. Plaintiff, Roberta LaCross vs. Three Friends Winery. That one we know all about." I shuffled more pages. "State of Michigan, Wyandot County Municipal Court. Plaintiff, Roberta LaCross vs. Windemere Apartments."

. . .

I SKIMMED IT. It seemed that Bobbie was suing her former landlord for not accepting a state subsidy plan she wanted to use to pay part of her rent. I checked the date, which suggested this was why Bobbie moved out of her apartment while she was convalescing at Patty's house. She wasn't saving money, she was homeless. I moved forward.

"STATE OF MICHIGAN, Wyandot County Municipal Court. Plaintiff, Roberta LaCross vs. Buford Campbell; Hal Buckwald, et. al."

OKAY THIS WAS INTERESTING. I skimmed the suit and then summarized for my sister.

"DEFENDANTS, Buford Campbell and Hal Buckwald, pressured plaintiff into relinquishing her financial interest in the property at 165 Lakeview Terrace in Masons Bay. Defendants used knowledge of plaintiff's struggle with controlled substances to coerce her into signing documents while plaintiff was under the influence of said substances. Plaintiff demands return of her property."

I HAVE to say I was a little bit impressed. Bobbie used her drug addiction to her advantage. Take it from me, opportunities like that don't happen often.

Buford and Hal had a motive. Hal. It had to be Hal. He hated his mother, that was obvious. That might not have been enough for him to kill her, but add the lawsuit and you've got murder. How to prove it though? Obviously, I couldn't pop over to the sheriff's office and tell Detective Lehmann I had a new killer in mind. Not twice in one day. He'd never believe me.

And... all I really had was the lawsuit. Which was a motive, but not as good a one as revenging a death caused by Bobbie. Maybe I was wrong, maybe Hal had nothing to do with it. I needed to find some actual evidence. Honestly, I had no idea what that might be.

I must have fallen asleep, because sounds downstairs woke me and I was suddenly terrified that I'd done something stupid and rolled over on the baby and suffocated her. Or let her fall off the bed and end up with lifelong brain damage. But no, she was sitting up straight—something she was getting good at— and chewing on Bobbie LaCross' file. I got out of bed, took the file away from her, and then went downstairs. Happily, I'd managed, once again, to not kill my sister.

CHAPTER TWENTY-THREE

Lunch was grilled tuna fish sandwiches and tomato soup. Barbara insisted it was her turn to feed Emerald, which was fine with me. I had no real desire to end up covered in spit out Gerber baby food. Bev and Barbara had brought a selection of baby food for Emerald to try: apple, pear, sweet potato, peas. I was eating my lunch as quickly as I could to avoid the coming disaster.

Barbara had mentioned an article about the intelligence failures that led to the Bush administration claiming there were weapons of mass destruction when there weren't. That was not a great topic. Nana Cole bristled, and said, "People need to stop talking about that. I'm sure they had good reasons to invade Iraq. For security reasons, they just can't tell us."

That led to an uncomfortable pause. It was pretty naïve, and certainly something she would never say about a Democrat.

Finally, Barbara said, "Oh my, she certainly doesn't like peas." Emerald had just spit a spoonful all over herself, the high chair and even the table. "I'll try something else."

Bev steered the discussion away from politics by asking, "Have you been watching *The Apprentice?*"

This was the perfect question. Nana Cole loved *The Apprentice*—or rather she loved to complain about it.

"Trump wants the women to win because they're pretty. Typical man," Nana Cole said. "But they really should give the guys a chance. Otherwise, it's simply not fair."

"It's reality TV," I said. "Of course, it's not fair. It's meant to be dramatic, not fair. It's meant to make you mad. Otherwise, no one would watch."

"I couldn't get through a whole episode," Barbara said. "He's such a blowhard. Men like that are just awful."

"Someone that successful is entitled to a few rough edges," my grandmother said.

"Is he that successful?" Bev asked. "I read that he's a rich kid who got handed all his money. And he really hasn't done anything but lose it."

"That's not what they say on the show," Nana Cold said. "They wouldn't hire him to do the show if he weren't a self-made man."

I made a mental note that conversations about TV shows could be as challenging as conversations about politics, and segued into Nana Cole's favorite topic: gossip.

"Tell me what you know about the Campbells."

"Bunch of drunks, going right back to the start. That's why they lost everything," my grandmother said, then added, "Scottish, but you'd think they were Irish the way they drink."

"Did you hear anything about a lawsuit?"

"Well... she was suing that winery. You know all—"

"Other lawsuits. Bobbie was suing her son and her cousin because they got her to sign over her share of the property."

"Really?" Barbara said. "That's terrible."

"Doesn't surprise me," Nana Cole said. "Those cousins are tight. They probably ganged up on her."

"How many are there, exactly?"

"There are Campbells all over the place," Bev said. "But

there are still five on that original property. Bobbie's boy, Buford, Andy, Harlan and Dill."

More suspects.

"Buford had a crush on your mother all through school," Nana Cole said.

"He looks like he's ten years older than she is."

"You saw him?"

"Yeah," I said, not really understanding why that was a big deal. "Twice. I mean, he just opened the door a crack."

"That's more than he does for most people."

"He's agoraphobic," Bev explained. "People haven't seen him in years."

"How can you be agoraphobic in Masons Bay? No one delivers." I got a lot of stares. Well, it was a practical question.

"His cousins bring him everything he needs."

I stood up suddenly. I was only halfway through my sandwich and hadn't even touched the soup, but I couldn't help myself. I said, "I need to run an errand. I won't be long." And then I left the house as quickly as possible.

CHAPTER TWENTY-FOUR

I took the Escalade. I had a vague idea of what I was doing and my car, my popsicle blue car, which I adored, would be too noticeable against the snow. Not that black was subtle, but still. I drove to the Campbell complex and parked a few houses down. I could just barely see the main house and the RV.

What was I doing there? Buford. Had he killed Bobbie? Why did I think that? Well, first, he said he saw Melanie drop Bobbie off. That was probably true. He said he heard a couple of gun shots. That was probably *not* true. Bobbie was strangled. So why tell a lie like that? To deflect and distract, which you'd probably do if you were guilty. What else? Bobbie was suing him, so he had a motive. Something he hadn't mentioned either time I spoke to him. But then, why would he?

Seeing Melanie there was an opportunity. All he had to do was walk thirty feet across his own yard and strangle Bobbie. Could he have overcome his own fears to do that?

His fingerprints. They were inside the RV. Yeah he owned it, but still, he probably wouldn't go inside. He'd have other people take care of any problems. Which means his fingerprints shouldn't be in there.

I stared at the house. In the middle of the night, could

Buford have slipped out, run over to the RV, killed his cousin, and run back? It was possible. But how to prove it.

It was starting to get cold, so I turned the engine back on. I imagined Buford strangling Bobbie. I tried to imagine every single detail. Then, finally, I said out loud, "Scratches."

I remembered seeing one single scratch on Bobbie's neck. A scratch that she wouldn't have put there herself as she struggled... There would be scratches on his hands. Unless he wore gloves. But would he have? *If* he did it, *if* it was him, it was spontaneous. A snap decision he barely thought about. He saw an opportunity and... Yeah, he wouldn't have worn gloves or a coat or boats. If he'd taken the time to put them on, he wouldn't have done it.

I had to see his hands. But how would I do that? He wouldn't let me in, so I had to get him to reach his hands out. I had to give him something. But what? I looked around the interior of the Escalade. There wasn't much. Nana Cole made me clean it out right before Christmas. There was a paper soda cup in the cup holder. Empty. The glove compartment held a travel sized pack of tissues, some gum, a pacifier, and the four-inch-thick manual for the Escalade. There was a blanket in the backseat. I was considering going and buying him some dinner somewhere, when I noticed the bag from Fudge You! tucked into the map holder in the passenger door. The fudge I'd bought for Nana Cole had never gotten into the house. That would have to do. I leaned over the seat and grabbed it. Then I shut the car off and jumped out.

I knocked for a long time. Maybe he wouldn't come to the door at all. Would that mean something? Did he think my coming back meant I'd figured it out? Was there anything to figure out? Was I crazy to think he'd actually come out of his house?

I was tempted to walk away. But then I noticed the plaid blanket next to the stoop, under the snow. He'd put it over his head when he ran from the house to the RV. It would have been like bringing the indoors with him. I know that doesn't sound rational, but then it's not rational to spend your entire life indoors. And it didn't need to work. It just needed to work enough.

Finally, he opened the door a crack. "Yeah?"

"Hi Buford. How are you?"

"What do you want?"

"I brought you some fudge."

"Fudge? You brought me fudge?"

"Yeah, you know, you really helped us out. When I was working for Melanie Frasier. The things you said, they helped. So I thought I should say thank-you and bring you a little something."

"I helped?"

"Yeah, you did. A lot actually. Of course, Patty Gauthier confessing helped too. And then Brian Belcher also confessed. So it's gotta be one of them, right?"

"Yeah. It would seem so."

I stood there holding the bag of fudge, hoping he'd reach out for it. And then he did. He did! I grabbed his hand and turned it over so I could see the back of it... Scratches! A dozen or so. Bobbie had fought much harder than I'd realized.

Buford snatched his hand back and slammed the door. Well, that was that. He did it. Now I had to go and tell Detective Lehmann, and the whole mess—

The door flew open; Buford grabbed me by the puffer jacket and dragged me into the house. He slammed the door shut and then pushed me up against it. His hands were quickly around my neck. And then my hands were on his, trying to pull them off me, just as Bobbie would have. I wouldn't be able to; I was making the same mistake she made.

I was panicking, of course. A logical response to someone shutting off your airway. I had to be calm though, that was the only way...

Jamming my knee into him, I tried to get him in the crotch.

I hit him in the hip though, which earned me a "Umph," and not much else. Pulling my hands away from his, I moved them to his face, upward toward his eyes, then into—

God that was gross, squishy. I could feel an eyeball slide—

He let go so he could push my hands away. I took another shot at kneeing him in the balls. This time my aim was better and I connected.

Pulling the door open as he whimpered, I was outside in a flash. Ten feet away from the house I turned and saw him standing in the door. He screamed in frustration.

I ran down the crusty driveway.

DETECTIVE LEHMANN WAS NOT happy to see me. I caught him in the parking lot just about to get into that garish Subaru. When he saw me, he said, "What?"

"Buford Campbell killed Bobbie," my voice was hoarse. I hadn't expected that.

"You're fucking kidding me. This morning you said it was Brian Belcher, who, you'll remember, confessed."

"Yeah, but it's Buford."

"The guy who won't leave his house?"

"I think he put a blanket over his head and ran over to the trailer." Okay, yes that sounds insane.

"And then he drove the body to the winery?"

"He must have had help... One of his cousins maybe..."

Lehmann frowned at me.

"Look... he has scratches on the backs of his hands. And he tried to strangle me." I tried clearing my throat. Seriously, I sounded like Harvey Fierstein—which was fine for him, but not something I was aiming for. I was still young and pretty.

Lehmann reached over to move my jacket away from my neck and I jumped. Well, wouldn't you? More slowly he pulled the jacket back. I had no idea what he was seeing. I hadn't wanted to look while I was in the car, but I imagine my neck was red, scratched, possibly already bruising.

I asked, "Did they scrape Bobbie's nails when they did the autopsy?" Thank you, *CSI*.

"Yes, but... it hasn't been sent out for analysis. It's expensive. We've been considering it. I guess you just made up our minds."

He frowned. I imagined their budget was miniscule since most of the county thought there was no such thing as crime in such a charming area—which certainly hasn't been *my* experience.

"You should go to the emergency room."

"I'm fine."

"We're going to need photos of your neck. That was attempted murder, you know."

"Oh yeah. Um...There's a phone on my camera. I mean, a camera on my phone. I'll do it when I get home."

"That's probably not good enough." He reached into his desk and brought out one of those old-timey instamatic cameras that spit out pictures. "Bring it back. I'll need a statement. In fact, I need two. One for the Denny Hazzard thing and one for this mess."

"Okay. Yeah. I'll come in tomorrow. Or the next day."

AND THAT WAS THAT. It took me most of the week to come in and make my statements. By that point, I had pictures of my neck from three different days, and my bruises went from brown to purple to yellow. My voice actually got worse for a few days and I sounded like something out of a horror movie. My sister thought this was hysterical though, I would read her the labels on her food, and she would laugh and laugh, until Nana Cole would say, "Stop it. She's going to choke."

It took some doing apparently, but eventually three of the four other cousins living on the property confessed to dumping Bobbie's body in front of Three Friends. There was one innocent cousin, though I couldn't tell you which one that was.

And then, Denny's preliminary autopsy became available. Well, sort of available. Technically, only his family had a right to see it. They seemed not to have a problem believing he'd died of an overdose. They'd likely been expecting that for a long time. They gave their permission for Carl and Opal (and me, unfortunately) to look at it.

Detective Lehmann was kind enough to bring the three of us into his office and close the door. He handed out copies to Opal and Carl. Then said, "I've highlighted the important details. Your friend had significant damage to his arteries, which would have constricted due to methamphetamine use. They examined his heart tissue on a cellular level and found necrosis. During a heart attack the heart muscle quickly begins to die."

"So, it wasn't an overdose?" I asked.

"The toxicology report will take another month or so. But the coroner is tentatively calling it a drug-induced heart attack, which basically *is* an overdose."

I watched Carl's face. I could tell he didn't really want to believe the yellow-highlighted paper in front of him. He asked, "What if the toxicology report shows there were no drugs in his system?"

"Given the circumstances, that's very unlikely. But if there aren't drugs in his system, he still died of a heart attack. Which at his age would likely be due to his previous drug use, even if it wasn't the direct cause."

Opal seemed to be having an easier time with this, possibly because nearly a week had passed. She put her hand on Carl's. "None of this means he wasn't trying, Carl. He didn't leave you on purpose."

I thought he might burst into tears again, but he didn't.

Solemnly, we left Lehmann's office. In the lobby, before we went out into the snow, Opal said, "Thank you. It was nice of you to help."

"I didn't really do much of anything."

"No, you did," Carl said. Then he threw his arms around me. I froze, instantly. The suddenness, his heat, the emotion. I had to remind myself I was fine. Nothing bad was happening. This was grief, not violence.

Carl sniffed a couple of times then finally let me go. I started breathing again. It was probably recently having been strangled, and other things that have happened in the—I mean, Buford had been that close to me, his hands on my neck. I managed to stay relatively calm when it was happening, while I was being strangled, and then, well, it kind of showed up now and then. And Carl, being that close, it just—

Opal, who must have seen how uncomfortable I was, patted me on the shoulder and said good-bye. They walked out of the building, while I stayed there a moment. I felt a little panicky. I had a date with Edward the next day. What if he got close to me and I freaked out? That was definitely not sexy. I tried to convince myself not to worry. Sex was sex. I was freaked out by Carl hugging me. Carl, who I wasn't attracted to. It was awkward. That was all. I was making too much of it.

I spent the rest of the afternoon at thrift shops in Bellflower looking for a turtleneck shirt to cover my bruises.

CHAPTER TWENTY-FIVE

The next day, I was playing with my sister, making faces and fart sounds. She was loving it. It was around four in the afternoon. Bev and Barbara were coming by later to have dinner with my grandmother, while I went on my date with Edward. He'd suggested we meet at six for dinner at the Blue Rooster in Bellflower. I'd heard people talk about it; it was supposed to be great. Of course, I'd happily go to a taco stand with Edward. He was the kind of guy who made even fast food romantic.

Someone was knocking at the front door. My first thought was Edward. But it couldn't be... it was too early, and we were meeting at the restaurant. Maybe there was a change of plans? Or maybe he was eager, excited, couldn't wait to see me...

Emerald was tucked in my elbow, pressed up against me, when I opened the door. Standing there were a man and a woman, both in blue suits covered with thin black windbreakers. They looked like some kind of law enforcement, and they had to be freezing.

"Can I help you?"

"You must be Henry Milch."

"I am. And you are?"

"We're with the US Marshals Service," the woman said. "I'm Officer Petrie and this is Officer Tran."

I felt a cold finger on the back of my neck and knew what she was going to say before she said it. "We're here to bring Emerald Hounsell to her parents."

"Where are they?"

"We can't disclose that. They're part of the Witness Security Program."

"If they're in danger, then maybe Emerald should stay here." My mouth was dry; I could barely get the words out.

"They're not in danger," Officer Tran said. "And it's time for their baby to join them."

Officer Petrie opened her arms to take my sister. I took a step back and I choked out, "Badge. Do you have badges? And paperwork? I'm not going to give you an infant because you ask politely."

As they dug through their pockets, Nana Cole came down the hallway relying on her cane. "What is it? What did you do now?"

"They're US Marshals, they're here for Emerald."

"Don't be ridiculous. She's not old enough to commit any crimes."

"They say Emily and David are in the Witness Protection Program."

And then they produced the paperwork to prove that. I felt disconnected, as though I was watching a Steve Martin movie. But there weren't any jokes.

"Uh, I guess you should come in while we get her things together."

"You don't need to worry. We have everything she'll need," Petrie said.

"Do you have a car seat?"

"Yes."

"Okay. She's in a onesie. She's got a snowsuit, we'll put her in that."

"No, she's fine."

Officer Tran was starting to look uncomfortable. He added, "She'll be with her mother within the hour. There's nothing to worry about."

"My mother's nearby. Can we see her?"

"No, I'm afraid not."

"So, you're just going to take the baby and leave us with all this junk we bought for her and then we're never—" My bruised throat seemed to close, and I couldn't say anything more.

"Henry, just say good-bye," Nana Cole said. "There's nothing we can do." She got closer and kissed Emerald on the top of her head. "I love you, my angel."

Instinctively, I held my sister closer. "This is so wrong."

Tran said, "It really is for the best. She'll be safe and she'll be with her mother."

"Safe and my mother don't always go together," I said, bitterly. "Which should be obvious to you. Who are you hiding them from?"

"We can't discuss that." Petrie said. Then she reached for the baby again. "Just give her to me. Talking about this isn't going to make it any easier."

She stepped forward and put her hands on the baby, Tran close beside her. I wanted to fight back, but how do you fight back with a six-month-old baby in your arms? They pulled her away from me. Emerald began to scream as they backed away from the door. Nana Cole grabbed my arm and held tight. She whispered, "We'll see her again."

"No. We won't."

I shut the door because I couldn't stand the sound of my sister screaming as they put her into the gray, government issue Ford. I thought about going up stairs and taking a couple of Ativan, maybe four, or five, but then decided against it. It wouldn't work. They wouldn't give me what I wanted. What I needed.

Instead, I went into the kitchen and got a big heavy gauge garbage bag. I went around the house and began putting everything that had to do with Emerald into the bag.

"Don't throw anything out. Just put it all on the porch," Nana Cole said.

"Why? You think someone else is going to drop a baby in your lap?"

"Take it to the Salvation Army then. It shouldn't go to waste."

She turned and made her way back to the living room. A few minutes later I could hear her crying. I continued for a while, dumping the baby food, folding up the playpen, putting her toys in a bag. Eventually I stopped.

I took a few deep breaths to keep myself under control. I grabbed my puffer jacket, put on my boots, and left without saying good-bye. And then I just drove, listening to the wind as it came through the hole in my canvas roof. The sun had already set as I headed inland.

Who was I kidding? I should not have been surprised my mother snatched Emerald back. Seriously, what did I think she was going to do? I knew she'd come for Emerald eventually. It's just... Did I think they were going to live nearby? Did I think she'd come back and we'd all move back to LA and live happily ever after? Why hadn't I thought this through... Well, to give myself a little credit, no matter how many times I thought it all through I wouldn't have come up with Witness Protection. *Witness Protection?!*

Never. I would never see my sister again. She'd grow up somewhere else, with a different name, without a brother. Without even knowing she had a brother. And I'd never see my mother again. Honestly, at that moment it was the lesser of my concerns. I was very angry at her. And in the midst of my anger, I realized that never seeing her again meant that my anger would never change, I'd always be angry at her. She'd never apologize or make it up to me or understand how the things she did affected me.

I was on Turtle Highway heading out to Queens Way Mobile Home Park. Ronnie had offered me a raincheck on some thirties, and I was going to take him up on that. My face was wet; I kept wiping at my eyes. I didn't feel like I was crying, but maybe I was. My vision was blurring, and I had to wipe fast—

And then a deer jumped out from behind a guard rail, running in front of me. I slammed on the brakes, and for a moment I thought the deer might get by me before—but then no; I hit it. After a loud bending, crunching sound, I pulled over.

I grabbed the flashlight from the back seat and got out of the car. I scanned the area looking for the deer. There was some blood on a snowbank, but no sign of the deer. I turned around and looked my car over. The hood was bent upwards, the fender was creased, the bumper was cracked, the headlight on the driver's side pointed off in the wrong direction...

"Fuck, Bambi killed my car."

ALSO BY MARSHALL THORNTON

IN THE BOYSTOWN MYSTERIES SERIES
Boystown: Three Nick Nowak Mysteries
Boystown 2: Three More Nick Nowak Mysteries
Boystown 3: Two Nick Nowak Novellas
Boystown 4: A Time for Secrets
Boystown 5: Murder Book
Boystown 6: From the Ashes
Boystown 7: Bloodlines
Boystown 8: The Lies That Bind
Boystown 9: Lucky Days
Boystown 10: Gifts Given
Boystown 11: Heart's Desire
Boystown 12: Broken Cord
Boystown 13: Fade Out
The Boystown Prequels

IN THE PINX VIDEO MYSTERIES SERIES
Night Drop
Hidden Treasures
Late Fees
Rewind
Cash Out
Help Wanted
Kapowie!

IN THE DOM REILLY SERIES

Year of the Rat

A Mean Season

The Happy Month

A Week Away

IN THE WYANDOT COUNTY SERIES

The Less Than Spectacular Times of Henry Milch

A Fabulously Unfabulous Summer for Henry Milch

The Fall and Rise of Henry Milch

OTHER BOOKS

The Perils of Praline

Desert Run

Full Release

The Ghost Slept Over

My Favorite Uncle

Femme

Praline Goes to Washington

Aunt Belle's Time Travel & Collectibles

Masc

Never Rest

Code Name: Liberty

Fathers of the Bride

Sentenced to Christmas

ABOUT THE AUTHOR

Marshall Thornton writes several popular mystery series, most notably the *Boystown Mysteries* and the *Pinx Video Mysteries*. He has won the Lambda Award for Gay Mystery three times. His books *Femme* and *Code Name Liberty* were Lambda finalists for Best Gay Romance. Other books include *My Favorite Uncle, The Ghost Slept Over* and *Fathers of the Bride*. He holds an MFA in Screenwriting from UCLA.

www.ingramcontent.com/pod-product-compliance
Lightning Source LLC
Chambersburg PA
CBHW021155310726
48971CB00002B/642